TO CAPTURE A KING

Alan MacLeod

This book is a work of fiction. Any resemblance to actual events or persons, living or dead, is entirely coincidental.

"To Capture a King," by Alan MacLeod. ISBN 978-1-58939-725-5.

Published 2005 by Virtualbookworm.com Publishing Inc., P.O. Box 9949, College Station, TX 77842, US.

Manufactured in the United States of America.

CHAPTER ONE

CAPTAIN RICHARD CROMWELL took a last look at the terrain through his binoculars before putting them back in the case that was slung around his neck. The scene was one of complete desolation. Nothing grew here. No grass, no trees, no birds sang in the clear blue air of a June afternoon. Stretching in front of him was a black, cratered desert. Last year, two hundred thousand men had fought and died here, and the ground was still bleeding from its wounds. Cromwell knew with a sick feeling that it was all going to happen again.

Richard got down from the observation point, then made his way back through the trench system up to level ground where he inhaled a deep breath, pulling a packet of Senior Service from his pocket. The blue smoke from his cigarette drifted lazily into the air. The company had arrived that morning from Arras and he had made a point of coming here to look things over. All lips were shut at HQ but there was no disguising the movement of men and material into the Ypres salient. Came an unspoken urgency, a quickening of pace and command. A new offensive and from the look of it, the carnage would begin soon.

Taking another drag on the cigarette he ran his free hand through his longish blond hair, keeping the butt end in his mouth, he used both hands to button the top button of his tunic. *Always be neat and smart. Set a good example for your men.* Had been drilled into him in officer school.

At twenty-four, he was a very young captain. He wished he could think that it was his daring and bravery that had given him promotion, but in reality he knew that it was only attrition. The death toll of officers at the front was horrendous. In the officers club last Christmas of 1916, the rumor was that the life expectancy of a green lieutenant in action at the front was half-an-hour. He'd laughed it off as a joke at the time. That had been before Arras in April, now he knew that it was no joke.

Before Arras, he had had only a young man's hazy notion of what hell was; now he knew with an utter certainty. Covered in mud and blood, screaming along with everyone else, he'd grabbed a rifle from a dead soldier and used the bayonet in hand-to-hand combat with a screaming enemy who charged into their position. No distant rifle fire, no calm orders to his men, just jab and thrust and shout.

Every night he prayed thanks to the Canadians who had taken the ridge at Vimy saving him and all his men from annihilation. Captain Soames had died alongside him. Richard couldn't remember the Captain's face now, only his blood soaking onto his leg as he lay on the ground. A battlefield promotion later upheld by HQ, made him a captain with the privilege of knowing why he was leading his men into almost certain death.

Richard ground out the cigarette under his boot and started on the half-mile walk back to the tents. In the distance a car made its way down the rutted track toward him. His green eyes squinted in the sunshine. Was that Wilkins driving? When did he learn to drive? Richard stopped and waited. There were almost a million British soldiers in France and very few knew how to drive a car. The open touring car drew up to him.

"Sir! Urgent message from HQ. You're to report at once to Colonel French. The messenger loaned me this car to find you. He's waiting back by the tents to drive you there."

Cromwell wondered why the colonel wanted a junior captain. Had he done something? After packing his kit he climbed into the tourer.

HQ was in the manor of an estate at Cassel, ten miles from Ypres, about thirty from Dunkirk. Richard's boots gave a hollow ring on the floorboards as he marched into the former dining room, coming to a smart attention in front of the colonel.

"Captain Cromwell reporting, sir."

Colonel French pushed the clutter of maps aside, motioning to the sole chair in front of the desk. French was an affable old man of thirty-five, or thereabouts. He liked to play the bluff uncle to his younger staff who arrived and died with such regularity.

"Sit down, Richard. What have you been up to?"

"Sir?" asked a mystified Cromwell.

French slid a telegram across the desk. "Read that."

Cromwell read through the honorifics, down to,

You will immediately detach Captain Cromwell from his unit, sending him to Calais by the first available means. You will authorize him for first priority transport across the channel. The captain will be met at Dover and escorted to London. Further instructions will be given to him upon his arrival in Dover.

Admiral Mansfield Cumming.

Cromwell put down the message, his eyes met French's.

"I haven't the faintest idea what it's about, sir! Can the Navy do that?"

"Admiral Cumming can." French growled. "I'm not supposed to know it, but he's not Navy, he's the head of Intelligence."

Richard didn't know what to say to that, so he said nothing. French pressed a bell and an orderly appeared.

"There's a car waiting for you, Captain. You'll go to Calais. You should arrive in London by late this evening. A word of advice, from what I've heard of him, anything the Admiral has in mind for you will be both difficult and dangerous." He smiled, eyes tired. "Take care, Richard."

The trip across the channel was uneventual. Dover was crammed with troops waiting patiently to be ferried over to France, further bolstering his impression that a new offensive was brewing. Richard noted the difference that a year had brought. Last year, when he had gone over there had been an air of expectancy, almost excitement, a year later they were patient.

He was met by a bowler-hatted self-effacing man, when disembarking.

"Clifford, sir. I'm on Admiral Cumming's staff. He instructed me to give you this." He handed him a sealed envelope. "I have two seats on the waiting train, if you will accompany me."

Clifford took them to a First Class compartment with a reserved sign on it and they settled in opposite window seats as the train blew its whistle, starting off into the gathering night.

Richard looked at the man in the other seat, fingering the unopened envelope.

"Is there anything you have to tell me?"

"Only that I have arranged hotel accomodations for you this evening. I'm to see you there then leave."

Richard opened the envelope and read the contents, which were just as brief and cryptic as the previous telegram.

You will be at number 14 Wilton Crescent at 09.00 tomorrow. Wear your uniform.

Cumming.

Stuffing the envelope back in his pocket, he settled back with his eyes closed. There was nothing to be gained by speculating.

Richard inspected himself in the mirror before leaving. The hotel, just off of Sloane Square, had been accomodating, given it was wartime and manpower short. They had assured him that his uniform would be cleaned and pressed by the morning, his shoes well shined. Clifford had told him not to worry about the bill, it was taken care of.

Richard looked again, his trouser creases were knife edged, the jacket well brushed. Standing just under six feet, Richard Cromwell looked to be a good catch for any young woman. Under his blond hair was a long, lean face with prominent cheek bones. His green eyes were set deep in their sockets, his nose long, almost patrician, an even mouth often smiling gave him small laugh lines at the edge of his eyes. Setting his cap carefully in place he left for his appointment.

On this lovely June morning, he decided to walk. Wilton Crescent was just off of Belgrave Square, a ten minute walk from his hotel. The Crescent had an air of understated elegance, two motor cars were parked on the street, horse drawn cabs delivered and picked up passengers. Richard couldn't imagine anything further away in time from the Front.

Number 14 was a white painted house with black railings, a gate led down to the servants quarters, four steps up to the front door and a brightly polished brass bellpull. Richard rang and was immediately admitted by a soldier. He wasn't dressed as one, but Richard recognized the build and stance right away.

"Please come in, sir. You are expected."

Richard followed the man down a short hallway and was shown into a room on the left. He took stock as he entered, the door closing softly behind him.

There were two men in the room, both rising to their feet as he entered. Richard guessed that the older man must be Admiral Cumming. Perhaps sixty, with an almost bald head save for white wisps around the side. Bushy white eyebrows sat above fierce black eyes, all set in a red complexioned face. The other man was young, with red hair and a freckled face, dressed in a simple black suit and a black tie over a white shirt. Shined, square-toed black boots and the glint of a silver chain entering the fob pocket of his waistcoat.

Richard wasn't quite sure what to do as the Admiral limped toward him, so he snapped to attention.

"At ease, Captain." A low, rumbling voice. Cumming gestured to a sofa beside the two seats. "Join us and have a spot of tea."

Cromwell sat and poured himself a cup of tea from the pot sitting on the trolley between them.

"Captain Richard Cromwell, may I introduce John Kestrel." Cumming sipped some of his tea as the two men nodded at each other warily. "You have both been abruptly summoned here, for which I apologize, but haste was in order. I know that both of you are wondering what the devil you are doing here, and you will be told shortly. I have spent most of the last forty-eight hours combing what few lists we have looking for two men that have your qualifications." He looked at Richard.

"Mr Kestrel is a detective with the Metropolitan Police. A man trained in investigative work." His gaze turned to Kestrel. "The Captain is just what he seems, an officer in the British Army with wide travelling experience."

He put down the tea cup, giving Richard a frosty smile.

"You haven't been officially notified yet, but your actions at Vimy Ridge didn't go unnoticed. You have been awarded a decoration."

Richard Cromwell sat further back on the sofa in surprise. As far as he knew, he hadn't done a damn thing to deserve an award, no different from the others, just scream and stab to cover his fear along with everyone else. The Canadians had done the job, not him.

"I have been asked to find two men to volunteer for a mission." Cumming continued. He saw Cromwell's face and smiled again. "No, I *really* mean volunteer, not in the army sense. If either of you think that this is something you can't handle, you will be sent back to your respective jobs and no word of this interview will ever be known to anyone. If you accept, I will be in charge of planning and operations, but my employer prefers to explain the nature of the mission in person."

Right on cue, the door opened, the soldier in civvies stood in the doorway.

"He's here, sir."

Cumming rose and limped to the doorway, Kestrel and Cromwell following. They walked down the hall to another door on the right. Outside the door a tall, burly man stepped to one side and opened the door for them. Inside was a large sitting room with bay windows fronting on the street. Near the window, to catch the light, was a table with two seats on either side and a chess set displayed on the table. A man was standing, his back turned, his eyes on the pieces on the board. He had the white king in his hand. As he heard them enter, he placed the piece back on the table, turning to face them.

He caught Richard's eye and gave him a slight smile. Richard's breath caught in incredulity then he insinctively snapped to attention, bowing his head briefly. Out of the corner of his eye he could see Kestrel doing the same thing.

The man standing before them was his Brittanic Majesty, King George the Fifth!

CHAPTER TWO

"GENTLEMEN, PLEASE HAVE A SEAT."

The king gestured to a sofa and took a seat opposite, fixing the astonished men with a bearded smile. On the table between them was another pot of tea, the king poured out two cups and sat back on the sofa. Cumming was momentarily horrified then realized that the king was doing it with the intention of putting both men at ease.

"I know our meeting must come as a shock to you, but the Admiral assures me that you are the best men in England for the job I need done. Milk? Sugar?"

Richard accepted the silver containers pushed across the table, noting in passing that the king wore only one ring on his hand, his wedding ring. The formalities completed, the king gave a swift look at Cumming who had taken a chair to one side, then leant forward steepling his fingers in front of him. His look frank and open, man to man.

"I'm going to tell you a story, one that I'm sure you have heard at least a part of. This one is more complete.

In March of this year, a revolution took place in Russia. Tsar Nicholas, my cousin, was forced to abdicate the throne. He is at present under house arrest in a small village just outside of St Petersburg," He threw a glance at Cumming.

"Tsarskoe Selo, Your Majesty." Cumming supplied.

"Thank you. When I heard of this, I became quite worried about my cousin and his family and asked the Prime Minister, Mr Lloyd George, for his assistance in getting the Tsar to safety in England. Mr Lloyd George concurred and instructed our ambassador, Sir George Buchanan, to open negotiations with their present chief minister, a Mr Kerensky.

"At first, all went well. Mr Kerensky was willing and we were going to send a cruiser to Murmansk to embark the royal family and their entourage. I was daily expecting to hear news of their safe passage here. I heard nothing! I spoke again to Mr Lloyd George and was told that there were difficulties. He was reluctant to specify and I suspected that he was dragging his feet.

"My father and Admiral Cumming were friends and I knew him from his frequent visits to Sandringham. I asked him to investigate the situation for me." He looked at Cumming. "Why don't you continue, Mansfield?"

The Admiral stretched out his wooden leg and considered his words carefully. He was loyal to the king, but he was also a member of the government and, as head of Intelligence, also a member of the War Cabinet.

"It seems that Mr Lloyd George has decided that it would not be politically expedient for the Russian royal family to be given asylum here." Cumming told Cromwell and Kestrel. "He has instructed our ambassador to, *take no urgent steps to assure their safety*. In other words, wait it out and see what happens. He is also most anxious that Russia continue in the war against Germany and is not willing to cause any antagonism with the people who threw out the Tsar in the first place."

"Political expediency!" The king interrupted. "The Prime Minister gambles with the lives of a European royal family for the sake of political expediency?" He caught himself.

"I'm sorry, gentlemen. I have noticed over the years that politicians of every hue tend to delay whenever they can. No action is their forte. If anything goes wrong, it wasn't their fault. No blame can be laid at their doorstep." The king smoothed his beard with one hand then continued.

"Anyway, here is the present situation. Mr Kerensky, while willing, has to be very careful. His own situation is precarious. I have become tired of the eternal waffling of these politicos. It is time for a bold stroke!"

His hand slammed down on the table and he rose and walked over to the window gazing out for a second at the quiet bustle of Wilton Crescent. He looked down at the chess table, then picked up the white king, turning to them.

"Gentlemen, I need someone with the knowledge and the daring to go to Russia and bring out the Tsar! To do it secretly, without the knowledge or backing of any of our officials. I don't want to know details, that I leave to the Admiral. Anything that you need will be supplied."

He placed the white king back on the board and looked at them with a serious expression "Will you help me?" He gestured to the white king on the board. "I need someone to go and capture a king!"

Richard Cromwell and John Kestrel looked at each other then back to the king. There was only one answer they could give.

"We will, Your Majesty." Both replied. The king's shoulders relaxed, he came forward to shake both their hands, giving Cumming a grateful nod.

"I will have no further opportunity to meet with you. I leave all the details to the Admiral, but is there anything that you can think of that you might need from me?"

"Gold sovereigns, Your Majesty." Came from Kestrel. "In Russia today, money is almost useless for what we need to do. We will have to buy men, and for that, gold is best."

The king nodded to Cumming. "You will have all you need, anything else?"

"Yes, Sire." Cromwell spoke. "We will need a letter from you to the Tsar in your own hand. It should contain something of a personal nature. Something that is not general knowledge. To convince him that we are really emissaries from yourself. He must be suspicious of secret envoys and will need reassurance."

"A very good point." The king nodded. "I'll see to it today." He moved towards the door, then turned.

"You should both be aware that I am sailing very close to the wind on this. I am a constitutional monarch and may not interfere with government policy. If anyone in the government should learn of this, I will not be in a position to help you, officially at least. And now I must leave you with my best wishes and may luck accompany you." He looked at the chess set by the window.

"Bring back the king."

Kestrel and Cromwell stood and bowed as King George opened the door. The king's detective stationed outside, waited until the monarch passed through, then gently closed the door.

As the door closed, the men sat down again, their minds whirling. Admiral Cumming quietly poured them all another cup of tea, the Englishman's answer to all emergencies. His low voice broke into their thoughts.

"Before we go any further, you are both probably wondering what expertise the other has that caused me to search you out." He turned his gaze on Kestrel.

"The captain here is the son of Rafe Cromwell, a member of the diplomatic corps, now serving as assistant to our ambassador in Washington. Mr Cromwell Senior was previously stationed in St Petersburg where he lived with his wife and son. From the age of seven until he was thirteen, Richard lived in St Petersburg. He is fluent in Russian and knows the city well. He returned here for his schooling then joined his parents in Washington where he was attending University there until returning to enlist with our forces." He turned to Richard. "Have you returned to Russia since then?"

"Only once, in the summer of 1911. I joined my parents there and we made a tour. They knew they were leaving later that year for Washington and wanted to make a last round of friends and places."

"Now you see the reason I chose Captain Cromwell."

Cumming told Kestrel before switching to Richard.

"Mr Kestrel's grandfather was Ivan Kestrov, a Russian merchant who established an office here in London, later becoming a British citizen and changing his name to Kestrel after our hedgerow falcon. John's father inherited the business and took young John to Russia frequently, hoping that his son would follow in his footsteps." Cumming glanced at Kestrel. "Forgive me for airing your private history, but it is important that you both get to know each other." Back to Richard.

"Mr Kestrel chose to join the Metropolitan police where he has distinguished himself as a diligent officer and now, a detective. For the last year, he has also been working under cover for the London, Midland and Scottish Railway and is in addition, a union organizer." He stopped to gather his words.

"We are now in the third year of a terrible war. It is being felt all through our society, but especially among the working poor. You may think that what happened in Russia could never happen here, but it could!

"Trade Unions are becoming more militant and demanding. For the most part, patriotism has held them back, but if things don't improve soon, it may become really serious. Mr Kestrel has been our man on the inside in the Union movement. He has identified the real hotheads and revolution- aries from among those who are only sincere in seeking to improve the lot of the working man. As a union delegate, he is acquainted with many in other unions. Even more important, he has an entree into the St Petersburg Unions. Soviets, I believe they are called."

Admiral Cumming stopped for a moment, mentally reviewing what he had said.

"After much thought, this was the best plan that I could come up with. We need a man in at the top, in the society of Petersburg. There must be a number of people there who would be willing to assist in a desperate venture. At the same time, we need a man who can provide information on the worker's Soviets, what are they planning? who are the leaders? What is their attitude toward the Tsar? In the turmoil that is present day St Petersburg, information can be the key to success. Now you see why I chose you both."

Both of his listeners were still trying to take all of this into their minds. Vague plans were formulating, ideas being rejected. Cumming overrode their thoughts.

"I want you to leave here, go and have some lunch. Talk to each other. Think about what you will need that I can give you. Do you want to go as yourselves? Will you need other identities to change into if the need arises? When you return, I will have some files to show you on people presently in the area. I want you ready to go by tomorrow night. You will take the train to Thurso in the north of Scotland. I am having a cruiser detached from our fleet at Scapa Flow to meet you there and take you to Murmansk. It's too dangerous to go direct via the Baltic." He rose to his feet. "Go and make plans, gentlemen. I will wait here for your return."

Cumming must have used some signal, for the effacing Clifford was there to show them out into the other world of Wilton Crescent. A world where there was no war, where it was always 1900.

When he had closed the door behind them, Clifford returned to the room where Admiral Cumming waited. He gathered the tea things and paused.

"Do you think that they have any chance, sir?"

the Admiral tapped at his leg with his cane. He was trying to satisfy both his king and his conscience. He looked straight at Clifford.

"Not a chance in hell!" he told him.

CHAPTER THREE

THURSO WAS BATHED in a fine Highland drizzle when they got there. Yesterday had a been a busy one with Cromwell and Kestrel dashing about London picking up this thing and that for their trip and keeping the admiral busy as well. Finally they had got on the overnight express to Glasgow. There they had changed trains for Inverness and again for Thurso at the extreme tip of Scotland.

With the war, and the Grand Fleet based at Scapa Flow in the Orkney Islands, this far flung part of Britain was experiencing an economic boom. The railway which in peacetime ran twice a week, now ran daily, shipping men, supplies and munitions to the fleet. So far, they had done a fine job of bottling up the German fleet, but German submarines were another matter. They prowled the Atlantic and the Baltic at will, sinking anything that took their fancy.

In addition, merchant ships in protected convoy made regular supply runs to Russia round the top of Norway into the Barents Sea and down to Murmansk at the tip of the Russian Empire.

Cromwell and Kestrel boarded the light cruiser, HMS Grenville, at five in the evening on Tuesday, June fifteen. They were given a curious look by the CPO who showed them to their quarters. The old man, the captain, was muttering in his beard about being diverted to pick up two 'damn civilians' and to show them every courtesy. Making matters worse were his orders forbidding him to ask them any questions.

They dined that evening in the officers ward-room where they were shown to a small table apart from the rest. They resolutely ignored the glances of the off duty officers and quickly returned to their cabin and rechecked their equipment, meager though it was.

They had decided to go in on diplomatic pass-ports and use others for their stay. Cromwell was James Neame, Third Assistant Attache to Sir George Buchanan, British Ambassador at the Court of St Petersburg, or Petrograd as it was now named. Kestrel was Reginald Peel, his secretary.

"Do Attaches have secretaries?" Kestrel asked.

"I've no idea, John." Richard admitted. "But you can bet your boots that no passport officer or army guard will know either. Once we get on the train, Neame and Peel will disappear, hopefully forever."

After some discussion with the admiral, it had been decided that Cromwell should use the cover of a reporter for a respectable newspaper. Since April, European and American reporters had been showing up in Petersburg and Moscow in great numbers to cover the war, the revolution and the downfall of the Tsar.

Alexander Kerensky, the Prime Minister, had ordered that they be treated with all respect. He desperately needed the goodwill of the foreign press to legitimize his shaky hold on the government. After some checking, the Admiral had found that the Manchester Guardian had no one on the scene and Richard Cromwell would become Peter Pringle from the Guardian. There *was* a Guardian man named Pringle, but he was safely at Allied HQ in Paris where he would remain, unaware of his Russian trip.

John Kestrel was to have two other identities, one overt, the other to be used if the need arose. The first was John Redding, also a reporter, but for a small weekly newspaper devoted to the Socialist cause. It was also the name he had been using as a union delegate for the railway-men's union.

The second was a reversion to his Russian name of Ivan Kestrov. Up to date papers on this had been impossible to obtain at short notice. These they would get in St Petersburg through a contact.

"I can give you only one sure contact in Russia," The Admiral had told them. *"and he's in Moscow.*

His name is Mr Robert Bruce-Lockhart, the Consul there. He also works for me. He has agents in Petersburg and I am sending him instructions to have one get in touch with you there, bring you up to date and supply any papers you may need."

Each of them had a money belt with a plentiful supply of gold sovereigns and British and French bank notes sewn into the lining of their jackets in special compartments along with the papers and passports.

Before turning in for the night, they went out on deck. The sea was calm and it was still daylight at eleven o'clock. This far north in mid June, there was no real night. Richard leaned over the rail and he and John savored the peace of the night and the hiss of the sea beneath the ship. Each was deep in their own thoughts as they smoked a cigarette before turning in. They had agreed that any planning was futile until they found out more about the situation, but that didn't stop their minds from roaming.

"John, in all the rush, we never got a chance to really speak about this. It was all planning, no thinking." Richard turned to Kestrel in the gloaming. "What do you think about this venture?"

Kestrel threw the end of his cigarette overboard and turned.

"I'm split in three parts, Richard. One part, the patriotic Englishman, is proud to be chosen by His Majesty for this mission. As I'm sure you know, as a policeman I'm in a reserved occupation, not allowed to join up." He paused and looked out at the sea. "My father made sure that I was well educated and was disappointed when I joined the police instead of following him into business. This is one way to do my bit.

"Another part, the old Russian, is glad that the symbol of tyranny and oppression is gone and good riddance to him. Another part, the law-upholding, staid John Kestrel, thinks that I must be crazy to be on this ship!"

He leaned his arms on the rail and glanced sideways at his companion.

"What about you, Richard? I gather that you were in University in the States. What made you give that up and return to this arena of bloodletting?"

Cromwell threw his cigarette after Kestrel's and grasped the rail.

"I wanted to join up two years ago, but my father persuaded me to finish my studies first. Also I met a girl there, we hinted around about getting married but at the same time it seemed to me that the greatest event of our century was happening and I wanted to be a part of it. My father tried to talk me out of the army, but I was adamant, I had to do my bit. I saw action for the first time at Arras early this year and learned how small I was. Thousands of men screaming and dying all around me and I wasn't even scratched. I was one tiny little cog in a vast killing machine facing lots of other cogs in another machine. One cog breaks down, you put in another.

"This venture is a chance to do something. Something really significant! The odds against us are tremendous, but if we fail, it will be a great failure!" He lit another cigarette and gazed out at the North Sea. "I suppose that's why the young do these things. The excitement, the danger, the joy of living. Our elders are much too smart to do it themselves, they need idiots like us to volunteer." He laughed. "We rescue the Tsar, become heroes and become footnotes in a history book. Who could ask for more?"

CHAPTER FOUR

THE TRAIN FROM MURMANSK to Petrograd was crowded, even at six in the morning. There was no soft class, just grab a seat if you could find one. Richard and John had been waved through at customs with no problems. Richard doled out some money and found a porter to take both their bags down the train to a compartment where three men were sitting together. He had seen them in the customs shed and determined that they were also reporters going to Petrograd.

"We'll latch on to these three, John." He told Kestrel. "That way we'll blend in when we arrive."

They introduced themselves to the other three and were welcomed into their group. One was American, one French and one Italian. They were especially welcome when it was found that Mr Pringle and Mr Redding both spoke Russian. Their view was sought as to whether Russia would stay in the war, although the American, Lucius Bulloch with the Herald Tribune, expressed indifference.

"Now that we're finally in this damn war, we'll have it wrapped up in six months to a year. The sight of some Yankee steel will send those Huns running." Bulloch opined.

Two months before, President Wilson had declared war on Germany in response to the sinking of US ships. Cromwell privately thought that the sight of some German steel might have the opposite effect on their new ally, but he had to admit that the infusion of the enormous industrial might of America made the end almost inevitable. Careful questioning elicited that the reporters knew less than they did about the current situation in St Petersburg or about the Tsar. They would just have to wait.

Someone produced a pack of cards and the long day passed playing variations on poker and whist, reading and staring out of the window. The train stopped at Kandalashka for food then down the edge of the White Sea to Belomorsk and another stop. Everyone was tired and dirty. The only WC in their car had long since given up and the stops were welcomed. They steamed through an almost unbroken expanse of forest to Lake Ladoga. The last part of the trip was accomplished in total silence, all the occupants of the car asleep. They arrived at the Finland station in St Petersburg at nine in the evening.

Richard presented their tickets at the barrier to a young woman wearing an armband and they were waved through.

The station, a huge, cavernous place, teemed with vendors selling bowls of kasha, glasses of tea, and vodka. Old and young women selling bunches of flowers, bootlaces and probably themselves. Soldiers in various uniforms prevalent. There was an air of bustling determination about the place.

The newsmen, Bulloch, Moulins and Graziani, were guests of the new government and were being met on arrival and taken to the Astoria Hotel. Richard remembered seeing the Astoria being built on his last visit in 1911. It was supposed to be the finest hotel in town with all the latest modern conveniences. A young woman with a clipboard and gold rimmed glasses greeted them with some confusion.

"I have only three names here, can you explain this?"

Bulloch looked at Richard with an amused glance. "I believe the ball is in your court."

Richard stepped forward and gave her a winning smile.

"Peter Pringle of the Guardian in England. You've heard of us, I'm sure? There must be some mistake. I was hauled out of Paris and told to come here to assist Mr Bulloch, our papers are affiliated. I speak Russian and he doesn't." He waved grandly at Kestrel. "I met my colleague here on the boat. He works for a socialist paper and can hardly wait to meet the architects of your glorious new government."

Richard bowed to her and to Bulloch muttering to him, "thirty all, I believe?"

Bulloch laughed at him. The Frenchman and the Italian smiled and the stern guardian of the Russian Press gave in and added their names to her list.

From somewhere, their guide scrounged up two taxis and they left for the Astoria. They crossed the river Neva by the Liteiny bridge and over to the Bolshaya Morskaya where the hotel sat in majestic splendor on the corner.

The room they were sharing was certainly well appointed. A large bedroom with two beds, a small sitting room and even their own WC in the suite. At the desk, Richard had insisted on paying for their room, avoiding any billing problems.

Richard unpacked and put away his few things. He had brought only one case, but John had brought two, one of them very heavy. He watched with interest as Kestrel heaved the heavy one on his bed and unsnapped the locks.

"I've been wondering what you had in there, but I didn't want to ask."

"Think about it, Richard. We're here in a large city in the middle of a war. We know that we'll have to pay for any information and help. We have money, but money isn't the only thing we can use."

He eased open the lid and took out some shirts and socks. Underneath, Cromwell saw two neat rows of Scotch whiskey and French cognac surrounded by a large number of British and French cigarette packets. He lifted some of those out and brought out from underneath two slim parcels which he opened, exposing in each a dozen pairs of ladies silk stockings. He grinned at his companion.

"It's not always money, Richard. Many of the people I'm going to see would throw me out if I offered them money, but a gift of a bottle of whiskey, well that's something else."

Somehow, the sight of these prosaic things brought home to Cromwell what they were really trying to do. He also had an increasing repect for the Admiral. He had been right in choosing such an ill-sorted pair. John, with his police experience and knowledge of the worker movements would prove invaluable. He put off the light and climbed into bed. Tomorrow would be a busy day.

CHAPTER FIVE

RICHARD CROMWELL THOUGHT that the meeting room at the Tauride Palace was small for the ten or so reporters from various countries crammed into it. Security was non-existent, he hoped none of them were German. No one had even asked for his business card or letter of accreditation, forged in some haste in London. The press meeting was the first order of business on the list of the genuine reporters invited by the Provisional Government.

He and John joined their companions of yesterday for breakfast to find that Lucius Bulloch had been doing some work on their behalf and had managed to get them on the official list.

"They need us, Mr Pringle, they need us badly."

Bulloch had told them, working his way around a piece of toast. "We have a meeting this morning, where we'll be fed the usual bumf, then a short tour and then lunch with Alexander Kerensky himself. It will be most interesting."

John had expressed his regrets, he was already busy with another appointment.

"I'm going to see some people in the workers soviets." He had told Richard. "A soviet is like a union of people in similar occupations. There's about a dozen different groups will be represented at this meeting I think. We have to find out who's got the power and who wants it. It shouldn't be too difficult, they want the world to know what's going on."

It was a fine June morning, with a promise of a hot afternoon. Richard and the others took a taxi together to Shpalernaya Ulitsa in Liteyniy and the palace. Inside was a kind of organized confusion. One wing of the building was being used by the Provisional Government and the other was filled with a Soviet of workers and soldiers; both wings reeking with smoke, rhetoric and bluster, each issuing conflicting communiques. Richard assumed that John was over somewhere in the other wing.

The main speaker was a Mr Goldofsky and he spoke entirely in French. It took Richard a moment to remember that at the royal court of St Petersburg, French had been mandatory for two hundred years. Seeing all the others whipping out notebooks and pencils, he dutifully brought out his own and made squiggles on the paper as Goldofsky spoke.

Goldofsky was a short, red-faced man who didn't seem quite sure of himself. He had probably been co-opted for this and had no experience. Goldofsky was flanked by two others, one of whom caught Richard's attention. The man was tall, an inch over six feet and stood almost at attention. Richard guessed that he was army. There was something familiar about him and it took him a moment to realize what it was. He looked like him!

Perhaps an inch taller and about the same age, maybe a few years younger, with same color hair. The green eyes were different and the face a little longer, but they definitely looked alike. The soldier had seen it too. He had glanced at Richard, then back again with a stare that softened into a smile. His eyes went back to the others, but kept coming back to Cromwell. Richard busied himself with his imitation shorthand listening to the speech.

There was going to be an offensive against the Germans shortly. Thanks to the generosity of their new ally, the United States, a completely re-equipped army was going to move the Germans back to where they came from. A grateful nod was given to Bulloch sitting beside Richard.

In light of the new government, Prince Michael had tactfully resigned his command and new commander from the General Staff would be appointed this week.

A map of western Russia was produced and broad dispositions were outlined. Richard wondered about the security of this. He then realized that the

Germans already knew, it was no secret, you can't hide an offensive, only the specific point.

Goldofsky eventually wound down and a couple of mild questions were asked about troop commands. It was a makeshift army and everyone knew it. The officer corps was split in two. Discipline in some regiments was almost non- existent with soldier Soviets voting on officers and on field orders. Richard waited a moment to see if that were all then raised his pencil. Goldofsky nodded to him.

"My paper has instructed me to request an interview with the Tsar."

He had deliberately put it in Russian to see how many would catch the implications. Goldofsky's eyes went cold and he looked swiftly to those on either side.

"Citizen Romanov is not granting interviews to any foreign journalists." It came out flat, unequivocal.

"Why not?" Richard made his voice sound reasonable. "I'm sure that Prime Minister Kerensky would like to give reassurance to other countries involved in this great war that the former ruler and his family are being well treated and that the change in government will have little effect on its allies."

It seemed that Mr Goldofsky didn't know how to answer that and stepping down from the podium, led the way out of the room.

Trailing along behind the others, Richard saw his look- alike waiting for him in the hallway. He approached Richard and gave him a short bow with his head and smiled,

"Yuri Cherkassy, Mr Pringle. If I didn't know that my father never left Russia in all his life, I would be wondering if we were related."

Richard bowed in return, thinking furiously. It was a startling thought, this man's father had never left Russia, but Rafe Cromwell had lived here for a number of years. Could father have sown some wild oats?

"They say that every man has a double somewhere, Mr Cherkassy, but I think that we are only similar, not twins."

He laughed to take any suggestion out of the phrase.

Cherkassy laughed in return and took his arm, guiding him into a small withdrawing room off of the hall. Inside he closed the door and showed Richard to a chair in front of an ornate desk.

"My new office, Mr Pringle, and my new job. As I think you guessed, I am a former army officer, a captain in the Guards. I was ah, pressed, to take up this new post as liaison between the Provisional government and the army. It's funny, I would have guessed that you were army as well."

Richard slouched down in the chair thinking that this captain saw altogether far too much.

"You wished to speak to me?"

"Your Russian is very good." Cherkassy was bent on his own point. "You even have a Petrograd accent, where did you learn it?"

"An old expatriate couple in London. My father told me that if I wished to become a journalist I should learn other languages, so I chose French and Russian. So what?"

"Because, Mr Pringle, you are the only foreign journalist in this party that speaks Russian and also wants to see the Tsar."

"You are mistaken, Mr Cherkassy. Every newspaperman in the Western world would sell his soul for an interview and it is well known that the Tsar speaks both French and English."

"But what isn't so well known is that those guarding the Romanov's speak only Russian and any interview could only be held in that language."

Richard kept his face still while his mind raced. Was this his way in? The whole enterprise was doomed without speaking to the Tsar about it and establishing some means of contact.

"Are you saying that such an interview could be arranged?"

Cherkassy gave Richard a calculating look and leaned back in his chair. His eyes and expression were speculative.

"We are a country in turmoil, Mr Pringle. We have zealots of every description urging our long suffering people to one course of action or another. One side wants to publicly execute the Tsar, another wants him to be exiled. Still another wants the war continued, while others are vehemently opposed to any further involvement. These are dangerous times sir, and the man who fails to see the writing on the wall, may find himself with his back against it and a blindfold being offered." He smiled and offered Richard a cigarette.

"As a member of the officer corps it was my duty to be loyal to the Tsar; as a lowly member of the new government, it is my duty to carry out their orders to the best of my ability. Mr Kerensky cannot do as he wants, he is prevented by political necessity from sending the Romanovs into exile.

It occurs to me that it might help everyone if an interview was printed in the western press and picked up by other major papers. An interview that, if written correctly, might force Mr Kerensky to do as he already wishes and at the same time, be able to blame someone else for?"

Cherkassy drew on his cigarette and blew smoke towards the ceiling.

"It would of course be expensive to arrange, a number of people would have to be, ah, taken care of? "

Richard flicked some ash into the ash tray in front of him and kept his voice non-committal.

"I am certain that my paper would underwrite such a venture, given some assurances that it would take place. There are those who would take the money and deliver nothing. I am sure that you understand that my paper would need to see something solid in the way of a plan and some arrangement on partial payment before the event, with the rest upon completion."

"The situation at Tsarskoe Selo is relatively simple." Cherkassy told him. "There are approximately fifty people being held under guard. The family and their immediate attendants, ladies in waiting, the doctor and a host of maids, cooks, servants and so forth. The guards are under the nominal command of Colonel Kobylinsky."

"Why nominal?" Cromwell interrupted.

"Because he is in sympathy with the family and also because these days, you can never know if those in the ranks will obey orders. In March, I myself saw ten of my fellow officers taken out and shot." He gave Cromwell a cynical smile and lit another cigarette.

"I was saved only by having a blinding revelation as to the justice of their cause. Later, cooler heads prevailed and I was given this job. Someone *has* to run things! I don't mean high politics, but the actual nitty gritty of getting things done. The Soviets don't have a clue. They give orders and expect that somehow everything will be achieved.

"But I digress, the only people who go in and out are government ministers with questions and food suppliers. All are carefully checked. In a city rife with rumors, the guards are paranoic about an escape."

"What about yourself?" Richard asked. "Have you visited there?"

"Only once." Cherkassy admitted. "There was a problem with the guards and I was sent to mediate." He grinned. "Some of the guards were getting too friendly with the family so I arranged for a weekly shift change. Why?"

" The easiest way for me to get my interview is if I go as you!"

The chair behind the desk thumped to the floor as Cherkassy let the front legs come down in surprise. He looked thoughtful, then laughed at Richard.

"By God you're right! It would be the easiest way! No middle men to bribe." He stopped, got up and took a turn about the room. "I would have to forge orders sending me there. One secretary to take care of. Kobylinsky knows me."

He was talking to himself, figuring it out. He turned to Richard.

"Go back to your hotel, Mr Pringle. I need some time to work this out. I will be in touch with you."

The two men, so strangely alike, shook hands and Richard left Cherkassy's office hearing the man laughing as he closed the door. He strode out of the Tauride Palace into the June sunshine thinking that he had done a good morning's work. In one stroke he had removed the biggest stumbling block to their plan and found an ally, if he didn't know it yet. He recognized Yuri Cherkassy as an opportunist and possibly an adventurer. Someone who would change his loyalties as the need arose and as the money was available. If he did this thing for him, Cherkassy was hooked, he could use him again. As he walked back to the hotel, Richard Cromwell was surprised to find that he was not as nice a person as he thought he was.

CHAPTER SIX

JOHN KESTREL WALKED DOWN the steps of the East wing of the Tauride Palace. It was only eleven-thirty, but already he was feeling mentally tired. The day had started off all right. He had worn an inexpensive, plain suit, surmising that the people he was going to see would look at him with suspicion if he dressed too richly.

After making some inquiries in the Palace, he was directed to a meeting of the Transport Workers Soviet. The small room was jammed with about twenty-five harried looking men all arguing with each other. A dead silence came as he closed the door behind him and twenty-five pairs of eyes looked at him.

"What do you want, Comrade?" came a voice.

"I'm looking for the meeting of Transport Workers. My name is John Redding and I'm with The Worker, a newspaper in England. I've come here to report on the fine work that you are doing in the advancement of the worker's cause."

That earned him another second of silence before the uproar started. Seats were vacated and people crowded over to him to hug him and shake his hand. The din was awful. Shouts of approval and congratulations deafened him before one voice rose over the others yelling for silence. The clamor stopped gradually and the men returned to their seats leaving only one man standing. An older man with white hair and a beard.

"David Mandel, Mr Redding. President Pro-Tem of this body of idiots! We welcome you to Petrograd. Please come up here and tell us what you are doing and what is going on in the world outside."

Kestrel nodded to the president and the others and made his way forward to the front of the room. He laid down his brief case and turned to his now quiet audience.

"Please, comrades. I did not come here to make a speech, I came to listen. All of us in the rest of Europe are watching what is going on and wondering. I'll just sit at the back of the room and listen. I will be available later to speak on the struggle in Britain."

And listen he did. The interminable wrangling over proceedure filled him with boredom. For a bunch of revolutionaries, their insistence on Roberts Rules of Order was laughable. It took him twenty minutes to figure it out. These weren't the people who had overthrown the Tsar, these were what passed for intellectuals. The real people, the ones who were hungry, tired of relentless oppression and fighting a war led by incompetents, were outside this room in the streets, unsure of what they had done and trusting this bunch to lead them to some kind of new stability.

As the meeting ended, David Mandel and a few others approached him asking questions. He invented freely, giving them what he thought they wanted to hear. He asked them for local opinion on the Tsar, what should be done? They were unanimous in wanting him gone. It was Mandel who summed it up for him.

"Don't you think that three hundred years of mismanagement is enough? I give you the words of your own revolutionary, Oliver Cromwell, who said, '*Gentlemen, you have sat here long enough, in the name of God, begone!*' The Tsar and his family have to go, permanently."

Kestrel was invited to Mandel's home later that evening and promised to be there. He was beginning to get a picture of what was happening, but didn't know how it was going to help in his attempt to free the Tsar.

As he went down the palace steps, he saw Richard in the distance also descending the same steps, he lifted his arm and started to move in his direction when his arm was checked by another. Startled, he looked to his right and left and saw two men had quietly taken hold of him.

"Mr Redding, we would like you to come with us," one said.

With a hand grasping each arm, he was hustled firmly down the steps to a waiting car and bundled inside with no ceremony, a captor on either side of him. They went only a few blocks past the Smolniy convent and round the corner to the Smolniy Institute where was hauled out and walked through a side door into the building. So far, he hadn't said a word, knowing they would be useless. These were messengers.

He was hurried down a hallway and into a room where a number of men, all smoking furiously, sat at desks. He was held there while one of the men went into an inner room and closed the door. He counted six people at six desks. Five of them writing studiously through wreaths of smoke. The sixth was on the phone and John heard the words,

"I don't give a shit what they want in Moscow, this is how it's going to be done!"

The inner door opened and an arm beckoned. He was walked through, his arm released and the door closed behind him. A man was sitting at a large desk and another sitting to his left. Both of them were looking at him with curiosity. The man to the side of the desk had a round face with bushy brown hair and gold rimmed spectacles. The man behind it had receding dark hair, dark penetrating eyes and a small beard. He gestured with his hand to the chair in front of the desk.

"Please have a seat, Mr Redding." He said in fluent English. "I'm glad you were able to come. One of our men was at the meeting at the Tauride. He telephoned us of your presence, he thought we should meet." His hand gestured again to his left. "This is Leon Trotsky and I am Vladimir Ulyanov, usually called Lenin."

John Kestrel curbed his anger and sat back in the chair, crossing one leg over the other in a show of nonchalance.

"There really was no need to kidnap me off the street, I was coming to see you."

"Kidnap?" Lenin's sharp gaze switched to Trotsky who shrugged.

"An excess of zeal, Vladimir. I told them to go and get him, I forgot to say that he was to be treated courteously."

Lenin was a man who didn't smile much, he had little sense of humor. On this occasion he tried, revealing bad teeth.

"I apologise, Mr Redding. In our anxiety to make sure that you saw both sides of the story, my men were too enthusiastic. But now that you are here, I am happy to make your acquaintance. The only other journalists here are from the capitalist press who have their own agenda and their own bias to put on the news."

John reached down and opened his attache case, withdrawing a notepad and pencil.

"Well now that I am here, I might as well do the interview that I hoped to have with you."

He launched into a series of prepared questions, his pencil flying over the paper. Unlike Richard, he did know shorthand. The questions were all innocuous, designed to put the person at ease. Then he asked the two that he really wanted to know the answers.

"What is your party's attitude to continuation of the war, and what do you believe should be done with the royal family?"

Lenin sat back, smoothing his beard absently, looking at Trotsky, who shrugged. Ulyanov knew that this was his best shot at getting something favorable about him in the outside press. He had lived in London for some time and was aware of the attitude of the British working class towards the war. He could stretch it a little, but not too much.

"I do not wish to antagonise your readers Mr Redding, but this war is being fought at the expense of the millions of Russian workers who are giving up everything including their lives to prop up a monarchy which is rotten at the core. Our men are fighting and dying in Galicia, for what? I also think that the soldiers in the German army have much the same feeling. Given the chance, both sides would be happy to lay down their arms and go home."

With a progressive government in place, not one run by that lackey, Kerensky, we could all have peace and get on with our lives. As to the former royal family, they and their government have been fools and they deserve what they get." His hand smacked down on the table. "The rule of the Romanovs is over, finished! When we have a real government in place, they will be dealt with appropriately."

He left no doubt as who he considered should be the real government.

"You saw the banner on the wall as you came in? We have them all over the city, Leon designed it. '*Peace, Land, Power to the People.*' That is what we stand for and that is what we will have."

John thought he had done as much as he could for a first meeting. All that was left was to cement things that would welcome him back and invite confidences. He reached back into his case and brought out his gift, a very carefully thought out gift.

"I brought this with me from London, I thought you might like to have it." John said, passing the paper over the table.

Lenin's eyes widened as he picked it up and turned the pages carefully. He looked at Trotsky.

"Look, Leon. It's copy of Iskra! The second edition!" He looked back at Kestrel and this time, he really smiled.

"Where did you find it?"

Kestrel smiled back and looked suitably modest.

"A friend of my father had this copy in his attic. Knowing that I was coming here and would probably meet you, I asked him for it."

Actually, it had taken two of Admiral Cumming's men a day of frantic searching to find it. A copy of 'The Spark' the paper that Lenin had produced and edited during his stay in London in 1905.

In John's underground work with the unions, he had remembered reference being made to the paper and thought that Lenin would be suitably impressed and flattered by such a gift. It seemed that he had succeeded. Lenin got to his feet and shook his hand vigorously.

"Mr Redding, I am overwhelmed! I will treasure this as a memento of my early days. How long do you plan to remain here in Petrograd?"

"Two or three weeks, it depends. I have to see other government members and also speak with the army representatives and perhaps even an interview with the former Tsar?"

Lenin frowned at that and shook his head.

"I doubt that. Kerensky is keeping him close mewed up at Tsarskoe Selo and no visitors are permitted save those approved by the so-called Provisional government."

"But there must be those who go there?" John suggested. "A change of guards, food suppliers, the postman?"

"Why do you want to see him?" Trotsky asked. He took off his glasses and wiped them with a cloth. "He is a symbol of our decadent past, not our future."

"Partly because my paper would love to have a coup like this, and it would raise my stock considerably if I could succeed where others have failed. Think about it, gentlemen. An interview with the former Tsar printed by a socialist paper! One in which the writer would be suitably grateful to those who made it possible?"

Trotsky, the writer and propagandist for the Bolshevik Party, looked thoughtful. An interview with a suitably penitent Tsar giving credit to the Party for arranging it would send their own stock up in the West and would embarrass Alexander Kerensky. It was a good idea. He nodded imperceptibly to Vladimir. Lenin looked down at the desk and the copy of Iskra sitting on it. This man Redding could be useful to them, perhaps.

"Give me few days." He told John. "Perhaps I can arrange something. You're staying at the Astoria with the others?"

Kestrel nodded without expression. "*Got him!*"

He shook hands with both Lenin and Trotsky and left the Smolniy Institute feeling that he had done a good morning's work. He arrived back at the

Astoria and saw Richard sitting in a corner of the lounge sipping a glass of tea. He joined him and ordered a glass of tea.

"And how was your morning?" he asked Richard.

"I got a couple of things." Cromwell told him. "The government is a mess, but I may have an entree to see the Tsar!" He grinned at him. "How about you?"

"About the same. The Soviets are a mess, but I may have an entree to see the Tsar!" he grinned back.

Richard Cromwell saw a small glimmer of hope on the dark road before them. Perhaps it really was possible?

CHAPTER SEVEN

CROMWELL AND KESTREL COOLED THEIR HEELS in the city for three days. There were two cities really. There was St Petersburg, a hotbed of tsarist plots and wishful dreams for the return of Imperial Russia. Then there was Petrograd, a hotbed of revolutionary plots and more wishful dreams. Now that the revolution had been achieved, the various underground groups who had joined together, were splintering into separate parties remembering all the differences that had separated them.

Richard became friendly with Lucius Bulloch the American from Boston. They went together to a press conference held by Elihu Root, head of President Wilson's mission to Russia. Root had made it painfully clear to Kerensky and the Provisional Government the conditions for a massive loan. He summed it up for the assembled reporters.

"No war, no loan."

After the conference, Richard and Bulloch went back to the Astoria and sat in the bar. Bulloch had a satisfied air.

"That should put the government in it's place. They have to go through with this offensive. They can't survive without that loan."

"They may not survive with it." Richard replied. "Have you talked with the people in the streets? My colleague, Redding has. The shopkeepers, the lady who drives the tram, the engineer on the train. There is an increasing feeling for Russia get out of the war by any means and the hell with the loan! In the long run, it won't make any difference. With America in the war, Germany is finished."

"It'll make a hell of a difference to thousands of American, French and British soldiers who'll get killed if Germany swings her Eastern armies to the Western Front!"

Richard, who had just come from the Ypres salient and a coming offensive, had to agree with him.

"Are you coming with us to Galicia?" Bulloch continued. "Goldofsky has arranged that we go on a troop train to the front, we're leaving on Thursday."

"No, I've arranged a personal interview with Kerensky." Richard lied. "I don't know what day, so I have to stay around here."

He couldn't afford to be away in case word came from Cherkassy. Bulloch then asked him a series of innocuous questions about British newspaper life that he sweated through before changing the subject.

Richard escaped with a grateful sigh and went to his room. John Kestrel looked up from his task as he came in. He had been practising with a broad nibbed pen and the watery ink that they sold in Petrograd.

"Tell me what you think." He gestured to the sheets on the writing table.

"I don't know what I think." Richard said. "What am I looking at?"

"These are up to date resident passes and work documents. I was filling in the names. The Admiral's man in Moscow came through. I've been checking the post office every morning." He shook his head and grinned. "It's amazing. The Country's at war, this city is in the grip of revolution, but the post office is working just fine! The papers were waiting for me in Poste Restante. I'm going to be Ivan Kestrov, in the railway workers Soviet, who would you like to be?"

Cromwell shrugged. "I don't know, Piotr Schmal." It had been the name of one of his father's servants from his youth in St Petersburg. "Are there exemption papers there?"

That was important if they ever had to use them. They were both young and with no obvious defects. There had to be a good reason that they weren't in the army.

"Yes, we can fill them in how we want. Wounded in action, vital civilian job, whatever. As a railroad engineer, I'm all right, how about you?"

"Put me down as a clerk in the ordnance department in the Kastrup Works supplying guns and shells to the army."

"Suppose they check?" John worried. Richard shrugged.

"If we get to that point, we're dead anyway, these are just for cursory inspection. How about a safe house?"

"I'm going tomorrow to Vasilevskiy Island to look for a place. Somewhere in a worker area, but quiet."

"Just make sure it has a back door." Richard told him. "We may need it."

As they were preparing to go out for dinner, a sharp rap came at the door. Richard answered the door and was confronted by an army corporal who thrust a sealed envelope at him, saluted and disappeared. Richard closed the door and turned to John holding up the envelope and waving it at him with a smile.

"If this is what I think it is——"

"Well open the damn thing and find out!"

He slit the envelope open with his knife and drew out an engraved invitation! It read, in a delicate printed type;

Your presence is invited to morning coffee and a tour of the Peter and Paul Fortress tomorrow morning at nine am.

Please bring this card with you to gain admittance.

The Commandant.

Richard's face fell as he passed it over to John.

"I had hoped that it was the word on the interview with the Tsar. It must be something that Goldofsky arranged for us newsmen. I suppose we might as well go and keep up appearances."

"You go." John told him. "I'm busy finding us a bolt hole in the morning, remember? When we go down to dinner we must file those stories that we wrote for our editors. It will look strange if we're the only ones not sending copy back to our papers."

Cromwell got his first surprise at the gates of the fortress the next morning. He was alone! At dinner there had been a few other correspondents but he hadn't mentioned the invitation, he had just assumed that they would all be there. His invitation was carefully examined, he was escorted in through the outer garden, into the inner courtyard and up a winding flight of stairs in the central tower. At the top of tower, a short corridor led to a massive black door. His escort knocked, turned the handle and stepped back to let him enter, pulling the door closed behind him.

The room was huge, taking up most of the space at the top of the tower. It was sumptiously appointed with rugs on the floor, sofas and chairs casually placed around the room, all centering on a large desk placed before the mullioned windows to allow the maximum light to illuminate the desk.

There was a large, wing-backed chair behind the desk with it's back to him postioned for the occupant to gaze out of the window. The Commandant must like to look out over his domain. Richard advanced a few steps, thinking that the Commandant must not have arrived yet. A laugh came from the chair at the window and a figure rose from behind it and faced him. It was Cherkassy! The man laughed again and motioned to a chair in front of the desk.

"I couldn't resist it Mr Pringle! To see your face when you saw me!"

Richard sat and looking at Cherkassy's smiling face laughed as well.

"Quelle surprise! You are the Commandant of this place?"

"Just for this month. Kerensky rotates it. Someone has to run it, keep order and a safe jail should he need one. As I said he trusts me, but only a month at a time. This is too important a place to leave unguarded in case of a counter- revolution."

"And you had an invitation especially printed up, just for me?"

"Good God, no!" Cherkassy laughed again and opened a drawer. "I've got dozens in here. The regular Commandant before the revolution, was in the habit of having small coffee mornings for hangers on. I chose it as a method of getting you here with a minimum of publicity."

"And the reason?"

Cherkassy closed the drawer and walked out from behind the desk over to an armoire in the corner of the room. He opened it and drew out a uniform on a hanger.

"Try it on, it's one of mine. We're about the same size it should fit."

Richard stood up and took the uniform from Cherkassy.

"You mean—?"

"Yes. You're off to see the Tsar, right now!"

CHAPTER EIGHT

"YOU MEAN NOW?" Richard echoed, feeling foolish.

"Well soon." Cherkassy countered. "As soon as you try on the uniform and give me some of the money you're undoubtedly carrying." He pointed to a screen in the corner. "Leave your things behind there, I don't want anyone to see them and wonder."

Richard changed behind the screen taking some of his sovereigns from his money belt at the same time. He stepped back out into the room and Cherkassy looked at him judiciously.

"Not bad, walk around a little."

Richard did so and Cherkassy shook his head at him.

"Too damn English. You have to be more arrogant. Strut! Remember, you're a Russian officer."

Richard strutted to Cherkassy's approval.

"All right, there's a car and driver waiting for you downstairs. He knows it's not me, but he's being well paid to ignore it."

"What's my official reason for going?" Richard asked.

"You're going to question 'the German woman' on her traitorous activities again." He meant Alexandra.

"Do you really believe that?" Richard asked, pulling the tunic down a little. Cherkassy gave him a look.

"Of course not!" He sighed. "The Russian army is poorly equipped, ill trained, undernourished and badly led. We are losing this war. You can't tell the officer corps that it's their fault, there has to be another reason and no one much likes Alexandra anyway."

He pulled some papers off the desk and handed them to Richard.

"Here's your '*laissez passez*' signed by Kerensky himself and don't ask me how I got it. None of the guards know me enough to tell the difference except Colonel Kobylinsky, he's in charge of the prisoners. He lives there and is devoted to the Tsar. If he spots the difference, he won't say anything. I'll wait here for your return, don't take too long." He lit a cigarette and walked around Richard. "My God you do look like me! A fine figure of a man If I do say so myself!" He grinned and put the sovereigns Richard had given him in his pocket. "Off you go and remember, be nasty and arrogant to the guards, it's the only thing they understand."

Tsarskoe Selo was only about fifteen miles from St Petersburg. A complete village built by the Empress Catherine as an escape from the the summer heat of St Petersburg. The village was designed to serve the needs of the court and had it's own extensive grounds. Two small palaces, living quarters, shaded walkways, a small lake and all the modern conveniences that an absolute ruler could have.

Richard Cromwell sat in the back of the open touring car and tried to look haughty as the car drew up to the gates and three guards lounging outside it. His eyes caught everything as the driver handed the pass to one of the guards.

These men were sloppy he decided. Their uniforms left much to be desired. The man who took the papers hadn't shaved that morning. There was a general air of indolence that wouldn't have been tolerated for a moment in the British Army. He took note of the guard house just inside the gates and counted seven men sitting in the area. That meant at least seven more somewhere on duty. He would have to ask Cherkassy exactly how many guards there were. They drove to the Catherine Palace where the Tsar and his family had been living under house arrest since April.

Richard opened the car door and stepped out, his eyes counting the steps up to the door, seven. He looked up and saw the golden cupolas on the roof. He hoped it was paint because they wouldn't last long if they weren't. His driver, who had been silent the whole journey, drove the car away towards the gates as he climbed the steps toward the door.

It opened as he approached and a guard with a slung rifle stood aside to let him enter. He strode into a huge marble-floored hallway and was confronted with another guard who came to a sloppy imitation of attention as he neared. His hopes for a successful removal of the Tsar and his family were raised.

'If this is all they've got, a troop of boy scouts could get them out!'

He followed the guard down the hall to a white door with gold trim and the royal coat of arms painted on it. The guard opened the door and he stepped in. Inside a uniformed middle-aged man with a white beard swung round to greet him as he entered.

"Good morning, Yuri Pavlovich, more of this eternal questioning I assume?"

Cromwell snapped to attention. This must be Colonel Kobylinsky. This could be tricky, he didn't know the relationship between Cherkassy and the colonel. Were they friends, or just brother officers in a tricky situation?

"Yes, colonel, one or two that they hadn't thought of yet."

He tried to adopt the slight drawl that Cherkassy affected. Kobylinsky came towards him and stopped, his bright black eyes squinting.

"What have you been up to, Cherkassy? You've changed. You look more military than usual, and there's something else, I don't know what." He shrugged. "No matter, He's in there waiting for you." He nodded to a smaller door at the end of the salon. "Come and see me when you're done, I want to make some changes around here and I need your help."

Richard nodded, not trusting himself to speak and walked to the smaller door and went inside.

Tsar Nicholas, former Emperor of all the Russias, was sitting on a divan smoking a cigarette. Richard had heard that he was a chain smoker. The Tsar came to his feet as Richard entered and Cromwell was immediately struck by how much he resembled his cousin, King George. The same height, beard and eyes.

It suddenly struck him as funny. Now there were four of them! Two sets of twins! It was beginning to resemble something by Gilbert and Sullivan. A movement caught his eye and he saw another guard straightening himself up from the far wall. That would never do.

He nodded briefly to the Tsar. "Comrade Romanov." and strode over to the guard who looked at him blankly. His green eyes raked the hapless guard up and down a sneering expression became evident.

"You call yourself a soldier? You horrible, disgusting little man!" He barked. "Look at this uniform, it hasn't been washed in weeks, you stink! When did you last shave? Get out of here, clean up and put yourself on report along with the other guard outside! If I see either of you again, you'll be at the front on the first train!"

The stunned guard pulled himself into some kind of attention, saluted and shambled out wondering what had hit him. As the door closed behind him, Richard turned to the Tsar and bowed. "Your Majesty."

Nicholas, his eyes twinkling, put out his cigarette and waved a hand at the closed door.

"Congratulations, Captain! I've been longing to do that for weeks. It's nice to see that there is still some discipline left in the army, I thought it had disappeared. It's Cherkassy, isn't it? what do you need to know?"

Richard took a deep breath and switched to English.

"No, Your Majesty, my name is Richard Cromwell. I am a captain in the British Army and I have come here at the request of your cousin, King George of England."

Nicholas stood quite still. His hand, which had been reaching for another cigarette, halted and his [illegible] watchful.

"You have some proof of this?"

Richard opened the top of his tunic and reached inside to pull off the tape that had held the letter concealed on his body all the way from London. He pulled it out and handed it to the Tsar who examined it carefully, noting that the royal seal on the flap remained unbroken. Nicholas opened the letter and read it swiftly, smiling at some reference made. He finished it and giving Richard a steady look, offered it back to him. Richard held up a hand,

"No Sire, keep it and burn it at the first chance."

The Tsar nodded and slipped the letter into a side pocket.

"My cousin is worried for my safety. In his letter, he says that he has sent you to effect an escape if possible. I am cut off from much information here. Why am I in danger? Mr Kerensky assures me that he will send all of us away as soon as he can. He tried earlier to send us to Britain, but something went wrong and now he is going to send us to Livadia on the Black Sea. In a month or so, he says."

"I regret Your Majesty that Mr Kerensky cannot be completely trusted. The various worker's Soviets here in Petrograd are totally against your leaving the area. His hold on the government is precarious, there is a great deal of turmoil out there. When he is ready, he may not be in a position to do anything."

"Do you have a plan, Captain? I must tell you that I have been approached through letters, by several loyal gentlemen who proffered assistance, but their schemes seemed to me to be hatched in some fantasy world."

"As yet, I have no plan, majesty. This is a reconnaissance mission to apprise you of our presence and to find out the situation. If I can come up with something, will you go?"

Nicholas wasn't slow on the uptake.

"You said, '*our presence,*' are there more of you?"

"One other, a man named John Kestrel. He also may be able to gain admittance to you. He is posing as a reporter named John Redding. But I doubt that either of us will get more than one opportunity to see you. When he comes, he will be bringing whatever plan we can come up with. I must ask you again, will you go?"

Nicholas lit another cigarette and dropped the match in an overflowing ashtray. He looked at himself in reflection in a gilt mirror on the wall then back to Richard.

"My wife and I have discussed this several times, Captain. We came to a decision. We all go or no one goes. I will not leave my family to the tender mercies of an angry provisional government, or any other government for that matter."

Cromwell realized that he had little or no choice. Trying to get seven people out of a guarded palace without anyone noticing would be damn near impossible. There had to be a way!

"Only the seven of you, Sire. No servants, no aides, only you seven."

Nicholas inclined his head in acceptance of this.

"I understand. I am reluctant to leave those who have been so loyal, but I can see the problem. Seven are difficult enough without any more. My son is ill, though. He would need to be carried, and carried carefully. Please put any gymnastics out of you plans. We cannot climb fences or swim moats!"

He smiled to make sure that Richard knew that he was joking.

Cromwell rose from his chair and took a few paces around the room, thinking furiously. He did not know how much time he would have before they were interrupted.

"What can you tell me about this place, Your Majesty? How many rooms? How many exits? Is there a cellar? Does it have an exit? How close are you guarded? Can you leave your rooms without notice?"

Nicholas held up a hand to stem the flood of questions.

"I can do better than that. We are presently in what used to be the library of this palace. Follow me."

He led the way to a long, low cabinet against one wall. It had a series of drawers which he began to pull out, one after the other.

"I know it's here somewhere, Ah! Here it is!" He turned with a rolled up sheet and gave it to Richard. "This is a plan of the building showing all the exits and all the rooms, even the secret ones."

"The secret ones? There are secret passages here?"

"Oh yes." Nicholas chuckled. "This place was built by my ancestor, Catherine who was known for her dalliances with some of her guardsmen. It was also an age when secret meetings were very popular. A private entrance known only to a few was essential in those days. But put any thought of using those out of your head, captain. They aren't secret any longer. The only one with an exit to the park was bricked up long ago by my father who feared assassination, and my captors are undoubtedly familiar with their presence. Take this plan with you and study it, it may give you a better idea of how to go about it."

Richard took the palace map and folded it away inside the case he had brought with him. There didn't seem to be anything more to say. They had been alone for almost half an hour, more than he had hoped for.

"Please say nothing to anyone save your wife, Sire. I understand that the colonel in charge of the guards is sympathetic, but it would not do to strain his loyalties too much. I will take my leave of you now."

Nicholas strode over to him and took his hand, then changed it to a warm Russian embrace.

"I cannot tell you how much of a tonic your visit has meant to me and also to my family. Sunny will be overjoyed to know that at least something is being done! Even if you decide that the difficulties are too enormous, we will always be grateful. Please give my warmest regards to Cousin George if you see him before I do."

Richard bowed and walked to the door. He turned with his hand on the handle to see the Tsar, his head wreathed in smoke, gazing at him with deep soulful eyes that now seemed to have a spark of hope in them.

Walking in the hallway towards the entrance door, he noticed that the guard that he had bawled out was nowhere to be seen and the other had now straightened his uniform and his boots shone. He smiled to himself. On the steps outside, he looked around for his driver and saw him hastening to the car at the entrance to the palace. He could still feel the hair on the nape of his neck rising. He was in enemy country, one false move or one wrong word spoken and,—damn! He had forgotten Colonel Kobylinsky! He was supposed to report to him before he left. He thought he would just leave and let Cherkassy think up some excuse if the Colonel got shitty about it. It was nice being able to let someone else take the blame, but he would have to remember to let Cherkassy know about it. He drove out of the palace grounds and through the village of Tsarskoe Selo on the road back to St Petersburg. All in all, it had been a pretty good morning.

CHAPTER NINE

THE LAST DAY OF JUNE passed with both men in a fever of impatience. They only had two dates to work with, July 16 and August 16. On both these dates the cruiser Grenville would be at Murmansk making a regular delivery. The captain would be carrying orders to keep a special watch for the hopeful arrival of the two men that he had carried to Murmansk in June. They might be accompanied by a small party. Every effort was to be made, including force, to ensure the safety of the party should they arrive.

Cromwell and Kestrel spent two days examining and discarding numerous plans to make the escape. The plan of the Catherine Palace was gone over again and again until both of them could have walked through it blindfold.

John Kestrel kept up his meetings with all the political camps. David Mandel and he became friends and he dined twice at his house. Lenin and his entourage were not neglected. He strolled in and out of their headquarters at the Smolniy Institute with impunity and on a few occasions had sat quietly, unnoticed in a corner while future policy was discussed.

"Of all the parties, the Bolsheviks worry me the most." John told Richard. "They have a ruthless dedication to their cause that appalls me. They will steal, murder, foment war, stop war, anything that will get them into power. But I think that my friend Vladimir is going to get me in to see the Tsar in a day or two. He told me today to stay available on a moment's notice. We have to come up with something before then."

He grinned at Richard. "I'm also planning a little surprise for him. Mandel introduced me to the printer who does all their work for them, mostly for free. He's in bad need of money and I've given him a little job to do, some headlined notepaper to run off. Do you speak German?"

"Very little." Cromwell confessed. "Just enough to say, *'Hands up or I'll shoot your balls off.'* Why? Do you need a German speaker? I can probably find someone through Yuri if the price is right. I assume that what you have in mind should be kept very quiet."

"What I have in mind for Lenin is rotten and downright dirty but then, it couldn't happen to a nicer man. We may not have to use it, but I want it ready if we need it."

He wouldn't say any more about it but smiled like the cat that had lapped up the cream.

Richard too, had expanded his acquaintances in the city. He noted with amusement that in a city rife with conspiracy, they had blended right in. He had seen Cherkassy on a number of occasions socially, using him to gain some entree into the life of the upper classes.

With some cynicism, he suspected that Cherkassy was trying to use him at the same time. Gentle probing questions of life in England. Once after an immense amount of vodka had been consumed, Cherkassy confessed that he might like a job as Russian advisor to the British army, or any army for that matter. Richard had taken to wearing a false moustache when meeting Cherkassy, much to the latter's amusement.

"I think it's in your interest, Yuri." Cromwell admonished him. "We don't want any comment made on our similarity, it may not be good for you if certain events should come to light."

Richard had hinted lightly that in the future, he might wish to employ the services of a daring gentleman with money being no object. He created a hazy picture of himself as being perhaps something more than a simple reporter and as having strong connections in the British government. It was risking exposure, but he was finding out that being a spy and getting anything done involved exposing himself to someone. All in all, he would rather deal with an amiable rogue who was in it strictly for the money than any of the Imperialist zealots who did everything but print up their plans in the newspaper.

The evening of July 4, they went together to the ballet at the Maryinsky Theatre. Tamara Karsavina was dancing in Les Sylphides. It became a shortened performance. At the beginning of the second scene, the house manager came on stage and quietened the orchestra. The house lights came up and the manager stepped to the front of the stage and cleared his throat.

"Ladies and Gentlemen, I am sorry to interrupt this performance, but urgent news has just reached the city." He paused leaving the audience in suspense. What new disaster had befallen? "Our troops in Galicia have launched a new offensive against the German army. As of this evening, our forces have been victorious! The enemy has been smashed and is reeling backwards in total disarray!"

There was a second's silence before the audience erupted in a roar of cheering. Men and women, total strangers, hugged each other in joy. The din was enormous. Richard and Yuri joined with others around them in the celebration. The rest of the performance was cancelled and Miss Karsavina was left forlorn on the stage. No one much liked Les Sylphides anyway and Chopin was Polish.

Richard and Yuri stopped in two cafes on the way back to the hotel. By now, the whole city had heard and had come alive. The streets were thronged in the warm July evening, people were carousing in the middle of the street nimbly avoiding the traffic. One tram, bell clanging, passed them filled with merrymakers shouting out of the windows. They must have taken over the tram. Cherkassy waved him a drunken goodbye at the door of the Astoria and Richard, somewhat the worse for wear himself, ignored the party going on in the hotel and went to his room.

In the morning, nursing a hangover, he made his way to the dining room for some black coffee. John was already off in the city. He read the paper with all the latest news and was just finishing his coffee when John returned and sat down beside him.

"You look somewhat hungover." Kestrel observed.

"Me and most of the population of St Petersburg." Richard responded, putting down his cup.

"Not over at the Smolniy Institute" John told him. "I've just come from there. It's all gloom and doom at the headquarters of the Bolshevik Party. Getting Russia out of the war is the linchpin of their platform. You can't foment dissent when Russia has just won a victory."

"I wouldn't be too sure about that." Richard told him, folding the front of the paper for Kestrel to read. "I'm a soldier and I've been in battle. If you read this carefully, you'll see that they haven't won a victory, they've gained some ground and given the Germans a bloody nose, but that's all. Give them some time to regroup and the Germans will be back, that's when it will count.

"This could be a blessing for us, though. Kerensky could take our mission out of our hands right now if he chooses. There will never be a better time for him to send the Tsar away. His opponents are silenced. Let's give him a few days to act before we go ahead."

"What do mean, go ahead? You've come up with something?"

Richard glanced around him, no one was paying any attention.

"Let's go up to the room and talk. There must have been something in the vodka last night."

In the room, Richard got out the map of the palace and spread it on the table.

"It's amazing how the mind works. We've been thinking hard and nothing came to us. I just glanced at it this morning, and it came to me! It was one of the first thoughts that I had when I met with the Tsar. I thought that it would be impossible to take seven people out of there with no one noticing. And that's what has been holding us up!" He pointed to the crosses they had made on the map. "Here are the guards inside and here are the ones outside. At night, the outside ones patrol the perimeter and are at the gate. They are not in close communication with the guards inside except when the shift is changed. We know that they are lazy and sloppy, we take advantage of that."

"How?" John asked him skeptically.

Richard told him and John's mouth dropped open. "You're crazy! It'll never work!"

"Why not?" asked Richard reasonably. "Take five minutes to think about it, then play the devil's advocate. Show me any major stumbling block. It carries a risk, yes, but we have to take some risk. We can use Yuri to hire some people he can trust, three should do it. If we can do it the night of the 14th, we can be in Murmansk by the 16th and on board and off to England. The pursuit will be hard, but it can be done."

John Kestrel took the five minutes and came back with three major objections. They discussed them fully and found the answers. They made a list of the things they would need and Cromwell packed the map away before they went downstairs. The place was almost empty with the corres-pondents still away at the front. The bar was empty and Richard went behind the counter to pour them both a celebratory drink. They raised their glasses and grinned at each other. My God, perhaps they really could do it!

CHAPTER TEN

THE NEXT DAY WAS A BUSY ONE for both of them. John went off to arrange the transportation they would need and he went in search of Cherkassy. At 24, Richard had no experience in corrupting people or suborning treason. He wasn't sure what he would do if Yuri turned him down. John would be better at this, but Yuri was his contact. He didn't know if he had the nerve to kill him. He didn't possess a gun, but he had thoughtfully included a long bladed hunting knife with his things. He strapped the sheathed knife around his leg before he went out. In the warm July weather, he would stand out if he wore a coat.

In the event, it didn't matter. Cherkassy was nowhere to be found. His term at the Peter and Paul was over and he had not been assigned a new post. Cromwell left Cherkassy's lodgings and took the tram back to the Astoria. He would make some delicate inquiries at army HQ after lunch.

At the hotel desk, he received a surprise along withis room key. A letter had been left for him!

Richard took a seat in the foyer and turned the envelope over. It had only his name on it. He tore it open to find a single sheet of hotel stationery. It was a brief note in English.

Dear Peter,

I've made it at last! Sorry to have missed you this morning. I tried to phone, but the system here is as bad as in Moscow. I'll be in front of the Admiralty building at two if you can make it.

Your loving Coz. B-L.

He folded the note carefully back into the envelope and sat back thinking, *'Who the hell is B-L?'* A sudden thought struck him. Could the real Pringle have a cousin in Russia? He dismissed it. He thought again. The only clue in the obviously fake message was Moscow. It came to him then. The Admiral's contact in Russia, Mr Bruce-Lockart! Something must be really serious to have caused him to make the trip all the way from Moscow.

He checked his watch, he had plenty of time before strolling over to the Admiralty. Richard assumed that Bruce-Lockart knew what he looked like.

"Delighted to see you again, old boy!" Bruce-Lockhart said loudly in English, shaking his hand warmly. They were on the steps leading down to the Neva. The river was teeming with watercraft. Tugs, ferries and a few pleasure boaters taking advantage of the afternoon sunshine. "I bring you regards from all the family." Bruce-Lockhart continued, taking his arm. "Why don't we sit on the bench over there and look at the river while I bring you up to date?"

Robert Bruce-Lockart was a small dapper man with receding brown hair and a moustache. He was warmly dressed for the weather, wearing a gray, three piece suit and polished black shoes. They sat on the bench and looked at the water for a moment. Lockhart turned to him.

"Sorry about all this, but it was important and I couldn't send anything to the embassy." He looked down at his suit. "God! I hate these formal things in this weather, but Buchanan insists on formality at all times. I had to manufacture a reason for coming to see the ambassador in order to see you." He smiled at Cromwell's worried expression. "Relax, it's bad, but not too bad. We have a problem, but first, how are things coming along? Have you come up with anything and do you need help?"

Richard turned to him then back to the river, surprised at his feelings. He was so glad to see this man! He hadn't really thought about their isolation until this moment. The knowledge that there really was someone else out there brought a sense of relief flooding in. He turned back and the green eyes smiled at Bruce-Lockart.

"We're going to go on the evening of the 14th." He told him and brightened. "Bastille Day! I hadn't realized. I wonder if that's lucky?"

Bruce-Lockart's gray eyes widened in surprise, then narrowed as thoughts came flooding in. He lit a cigarette and gave one to Cromwell. He hadn't been told much about this operation, only that it was a desperate gamble and that he should try to get the two men out if a wheel came off. He wasn't an official employee of Cumming, just one of hundreds that he used to obtain information from unlikely sources.

"Tell me about it." he suggested.

Cromwell told him the plan and Bruce-Lockart digested it in silence for a moment.

"Christ! You don't make any little plans do you?" He spoke almost in admiration. "I'll send C a coded message when I get back to the embassy. He'll flash a message to the Grenville to expect you. Which brings me to why I came here in the first place." He stubbed out his cigarette. "It's about Mr Pringle in Paris. C has just learned that the editor of the Guardian has, in his innocence, ordered Mr Pringle to leave Paris and make his way here to St Petersburg!"

"Good God!" Cromwell was shocked. "Can we stop him somehow?"

"All ready been tried old boy." Bruce-Lockart was sympathetic. "The instant he heard, C was on the phone to the Guardian editor to have Pringle recalled, but he was too late. He sent a man round in Paris to catch him, but he missed him as well. Mr Pringle is now somewhere on the high seas on the way to Murmansk on a French ship. We can't use radio, it's too dangerous in sub-infested waters and the French, quite rightly, won't release any information about sailing times or routes."

"So what do we do?"

"We pray. The other reason I came here was to personally send two men to Murmansk to stop Mr Pringle when he arrives and turn him round again. If all goes well, there's an end to it. But if they miss him, you had better be ready to make a sudden departure."

"When is he likely to land here?"

"That's a bit iffy. The ship may take a circuitous route to avoid German waters, but we think in the next two to three days."

Cromwell laughed. It was just like being in the army. Things got fouled up for the silliest reasons. It reminded him of a story he had heard in the mess. An offensive had been planned at Cambrai using these new tanks and the whole thing got off to a bad start because the signalling officer couldn't find a green flare for his Very pistol!

"So what do I do now?" he asked.

"You take this photo that I'm going to hand you. Let's say it's a photo of your Auntie Annie. On the back is an address. It's a private house in Helsinki. If you have to make a run for it, Finland is your best bet. I'm going to get up now. We look at the photo together then shake my hand and leave, putting the photo in your pocket. The first chance you get, memorize the address and destroy the photo and the very best of luck to you and Kestrel."

"One question before you go. Why all this mumbo-jumbo?"

Bruce-Lockart, who had half stood up, sat down with a sigh.

"I forgot, this is all new to you isn't it? Well, right now, due to the recent circumstances, this city probably has more spies in it than Paris, London and Berlin combined!"

Everyone wants to know what is going to happen. There's the Okrana, the old secret police, they didn't just disappear with the Tsar, you know. Then there's a couple of royalist factions, at least three revolutionary parties, not to mention the British, French and German contingents and probably a couple of others I don't know about. Watch your back! Now I really have to go."

He got to his feet and Cromwell followed suit. They shook hands after examining the photo and Bruce-Lockhart turned and walked away along the embankment, pausing only to admire the view before climbing the steps and heading in the direction of the British embassy. Cromwell remained for a few minutes before reminding himself that he'd better get back to the hotel and inform John of the latest developments.

As he got to the top of the embankment and the broad walkway, a car pulled into the curb beside him and two men jumped out. Ignoring the startled cries of passersby, he was grabbed and hurled into the back seat. The car took off at a high rate of speed and the scene at the admiralty returned to normal. It had only taken ten seconds.

The car, a closed black Daimler, manoeuvered quickly through the city streets with Cromwell being held fast between the two men in the back seat. They crossed the Liteiny bridge into Vyborg, a heavy working class area of the city. Rows of ancient tenements interspersed with small shops and light manufacturing plants.

Without warning, they made a sharp right turn into an enclosed courtyard. Richard was held in the back while the driver got out and closed the double doored entrance. The three of them then hustled him inside the building.

In the the dim light, it seemed to be a warehouse of some kind. There were numerous boxes and crates piled up in two corners of the room, a third corner was a kind of makeshift office with a large desk and several chairs. There was a naked light bulb suspended above the desk and behind it was sitting a man smoking a cigar.

He was of medium height, dark complexioned and with a large bushy moustache. His dark eyes regarded Richard with an amused expression as he was searched before being pushed down into a chair facing the man. His passport and wallet were taken. The knife on his leg was found and removed. This caused some significant looks, but no comment.

Richard was happy that he had left his money belt in the hotel safe. The man behind the desk stubbed out the cigar and examined the passport, his Peter Pringle one. So far, no one had said a word. The man put the passport down on the desk and looked at him.

"So, Mr Pringle, what are you doing in Petrograd?" He said in accented Russian.

Richard just looked at him.

"Don't you speak Russian?"

"Nyet." Richard replied. With Bruce-Lockart's lecture still fresh in his ears, he thought his best bet was to be stupid.

The man with the moustache appeared frustrated. How was he going to question him? His ideas on this were interrupted when the door banged open and another man appeared. This was the boss, Richard decided. He was tall and black haired with a pale aristocratic face. Well dressed with a tie and jacket in the summer heat. He strode further in and saw Richard sitting in the chair. He looked at Moustache.

"Who's this?" he asked.

"I was going to call you." Moustache appeared uncomfortable. "He's a British reporter, or so his passport says. He met with the Moscow man and I thought that we should question him."

"You? Think?" The boss seemed amused at the suggestion. "Why don't you start at the beginning?"

"We got a phone call from Moscow, you were away. The British spy, Lockart, was on the Petrograd train. I sent these two to meet it and see where he went."

"And he went directly to the British Embassy, you dolt. He's the Moscow Consul." The boss finished for him. He looked at Richard. "Why are you talking in front of him?"

"He doesn't speak Russian, it's all right."

Richard was looking at the desk and ignoring the conversation while drinking it all in.

"God, you're a trusting soul!" The boss said, sarcastically. He switched to speaking German. Richard didn't understand a word, but he knew German when he heard it. He had already figured it out. Bruce-Lockart had landed him right in it. The boss and Moustache were German spies, the others must be local talent. This was not going to be as easy as John's adventure with the Bolsheviks. There was more conversation in German then the boss came over to the chair and looked down at him.

"Parlez-vous francais?" he asked.

"Yes," Richard answered in French, "and I'd like to know what this is about. Who are you people? The police? Why have I been kidnapped?"

"We are undercover police for the Provisional Government." The man replied smoothly. "You were seen meeting with a suspicious person. Someone we think is an enemy of the Revolution. My colleague here, decided to bring you in for questioning."

That line was so thin a blind man could have seen through it, but Richard decided to stay stupid.

"An enemy of the—? That's silly! I met with the British consul from Moscow, he's my cousin. He had to come here on business and took the opportunity to meet briefly with me and exchange family news."

His interrogator feigned surprise.

"Really? Perhaps we were misinformed. I will check into this immediately. Tell me, what did you talk about?"

"Nothing much, family gossip. Who's getting married, how all the children are, the health of various aged relatives and so on."

"Did you talk about the war?"

"Of course, a little. The new offensive seems to be going well, I'm sorry to have missed it."

"What does he say about Britain's attitude to the new government?"

"I don't know, I didn't ask him. I suppose they support it."

Richard thought he had gone far enough. Even a dim witted clod would be suspicious by now.

"What is this about? Why are you still holding me? You have my passport there, you can see I'm British and a guest of your government. Mr Kerensky wants to give us a good impression, this is not the way to do it. When I speak with your representative, he will be very angry with you."

The man picked up his passport from the table and thumbed through it. He put it down and picked up the photo.

"Who is this woman?"

"My aunt, it was taken on holiday somewhere."

"And the address on the back?"

"What address? I never looked at the back."

"This one."

The back of the photo was thrust in front of him. the address was meatly written in pencil. *18 Vainugatan.* He shrugged. "I've no idea. Perhaps where she was staying."

"Very well, I'm sorry to have detained you." '*You are an English pig and I'm going to shoot you!*'

The last part was put in Russian. Richard did not let a flicker of expression pass over his face. He had been expecting something like that.

"Good, can I go now?"

"Shortly. We're checking what you said about the other man. I have to leave, but one of these men will take you back to your hotel."

He left the desk and stood some distance apart talkng with Moustache in German.

"What do you think, Gottfried, is he a spy?" Moustache asked. The other shrugged.

"It doesn't really matter one way or the other. If we let him go, he'll complain and ask questions. He's seen my face and yours. An investigation would find us. It's also a good opportunity to further embarrass the Kerensky government. After dark, take him somewhere quiet and shoot him. Mutilate the body and make sure that it will be found." He smiled. *"I can see the headlines; Foreign Allied journalist found brutally slain! What is the government doing?"*

He turned and gave Richard a reassuring smile before going through the outer door and slamming it behind him. Richard hadn't understood a word that had been said, but he understood what Moustache told the two men in Russian. Involuntarily, his eyes turned to the dirt grimed window. The sun was definitely going down.

The next half hour was spent in silence. Richard got up once and pantomimed taking a small stroll around his prison. One of them walked with him. What he was desperately looking for was a weapon of some kind. The shadows lengthened and Moustache told his two executioners that he was going. He left and Richard heard the sound of a car starting. Ten minutes later, one of his captors started gathering things together and left to put them in the car. Richard noted that among the things was an axe and some rope.

He was definitely worried now. His enemies had been reduced to two, but he felt that if he got in that car, he was dead. Probably the best chance was as they were leaving, a push and a dash for the courtyard door.

The other man had been gone for a few minutes now, there was only one man between him and the door, perhaps now? There came a sharp authoritative rap at the warehouse door. Puzzled, the remaining guard strolled over to the door and opened it. A large piece of wood came flashing down on his head with a crump and he fell to the floor. The door was pushed open a further and a figure walked in, throwing the two by four to the ground. Richard stared in amazement. It was Lucius Bulloch!

CHAPTER ELEVEN

BULLOCH SKIRTED the unconscious guard and grinned at Richard.

"Sorry for the delay, but I wasn't sure how many were in this room. It took me a devil of a time to get up on the roof and peer through the skylight. Once we got it down to two, I figured it was a snap."

Richard shook his head. "For this relief, much thanks, but how? why?—-"

"Later, Peter, later. Let's get the hell out of here and back to the bosom of the Astoria."

"What about the other man?"

"He's taking a nap outside, but we have to get going, I have a car around the corner."

Richard Cromwell sipped at his drink in the Astoria bar and looked at his companion in a new light.

"Do you want to tell me how you arrived at such an opportune moment? I thought you were at the front with the others."

"I was, but I took a train last night instead of joining the others coming back today. I was just arrivng at the hotel when I saw you leaving and I followed you."

"You followed me? Why? And where did you get a car?"

"The car, well, I stole that. When I saw you snatched, the only thing to do was try to follow. It didn't come to any harm and the owner will get it back. As to why I followed you," He glanced around at the bar. "Let's go over there to that booth, it's quieter."

Richard sipped at his beer and waited. German beer had been off the market for two years. Only an hotel like the Astoria could get the Dutch or French versions.

"As you may have gathered," Bulloch began, "I'm no more a reporter than you are. I suspected you and your friend, Redding, shortly after you got on the train. I've actually worked for a paper and there's just too many things you don't know about it. And your conversations with Redding when you thought they were private, gave it away."

"I thought you didn't speak Russian?"

Bulloch gave him a sincere look, "I lie a lot." He smiled. "But it [illegible], I heard what these two in the warehouse were ordered to do and I had to get you out of it."

"I'm very grateful," Richard said, "but why?"

"Because without knowing it, you have been doing some of my work for me. I figure you're army, right?"

Richard cautiously nodded his head, waiting.

"I assume that you are on some kind of mission for intelligence and I don't want to get in your way, we're on the same side after all. I've been sent here to do a job and your poking about has allowed me follow up where you have already been. Your Mr Cherkassy interests me. He might be the person I'm looking for."

"Who are you looking for?"

"All right, I'll put my cards on the table. I work for Mr Wilson."

"Who?"

"The President, you ass! I'm with the Treasury Department. We don't have the kind of Secret Service you and the French have, we're the nearest thing for the moment."

Richard looked around and ordered two more beers, this was going to take a while.

"As you and the whole world know, Congress passed a bill loaning Russia a massive amount of money to continue the war." Bulloch continued. "However, what is not generally known is we don't actually give Russia any money. What they've done is to authorize the spending of money on armaments which is sent to Russia. It's a nice deal. The US gun makers get a big contract with no risk that Russia will renege on it and they'll wait for a while to get paid."

"Anyway, last month the first shipment was made from the US to Vladivostock. Mostly small arms, rifles, BARs, grenades, mortars and of course the ammunition to go with them. They were all stencilled Medical Supplies for safety.

In Vladivostock they were put in a sealed, guarded train and sent all the way across Russia. First to Moscow, where some of it was unloaded, then to here. Of the crates unloaded here, about a third were neatly stencilled crates of sand! As you can imagine, there was quite a ruckus about it with both America and Russia accusing each other. Were the crates substituted in San Francisco or somewhere in Russia? Our people have been checking all the way from the suppliers in America to here. I got this end of the trail."

Richard wasn't quite sure what to think. Bulloch had saved his life and exposed himself in the doing.

"What do you think will happen now? About those two Germans, I mean."

"Nothing. When the leader comes back and they find that you escaped, I imagine they will leave the city in a hurry, thinking that you will expose them. What do you think of my idea of your friend Yuri being involved in my theft?"

"Why him?"

"Well, if it was done here, it needed someone to be either in the government or in the army to organize it. Your friend is in both. I've done some discreet checking on him. Did you know that he and Mandel are friends? He is also quite friendly with Zinoviev over in the Bolshevik camp. He is also seen frequently with a number of young, unemployed, Tsarists officers. He's very bright, well educated and has a finger in every political pie in the city. He's playing all sides of this game and is flat broke."

"I don't quite see the reason." Richard said. "I can see him cultivating everyone, he doesn't know who is going to come out on top, and is hedging his bets. But stealing arms,—why? He doesn't need them. What is missing, by the way?"

"Small arms, mostly. Guns, rifles, machine guns, dynamite, mortars and the ammunition to go with it. Just the thing for a small mounted force to wreak havoc. And he would need them,- as a bargaining chip. When the dust settles, there's only going to be one or two major forces left and he can sell them, with himself, to the highest bidder.

Of course, I could be wrong, it might be someone else, but I've combed the army lists and all the government people and he stands out as the the most competent."

Richard put what he knew of Yuri Cherkassy into the equation, it did make some sense.

"I sort of admire the man," Bulloch continued, "even if he does look like you! You know he might have been a General by now if he hadn't made a mistake. He actually told Prince Michael he was wrong!

It was back in 1915. He protested flinging thousands of men in a frontal assault against a superior armed force and suggested that he lead a small mounted force round behind the German lines to blow up bridges and rail lines then attack from the rear in concert with a frontal assault. He was turned down, and that was all right, but then he made his mistake. He went ahead and did it anyway!"

Richard nodded his head and sipped some more beer. That sounded like Yuri.

"It was a brilliant success! He created havoc in the German lines and it was one of the few successes the Russian army had had up to that point. It wasn't followed up in front of course, and the attack petered out. Well, the General Staff weren't going to let him get away with rubbing their noses in it and he was sent back to St Petersburg in charge of a holding company to be forgotten.

That's one reason I have him on my list. He probably resents being used and thrown away and it hasn't escaped my notice that what was taken was just the kind of thing he would need in a similar action in the future. He reminds me of one of my countrymen in the Civil War, Nathan Bedford

Forrest, a brilliant cavalry commander and scoundrel." He took a sip of his beer and continued. "I would like you to keep close to Cherkassy and let me know if he tips anything to confirm my hunch about him. as long as it doesn't interfere with your primary mission, whatever that is."

Richard took some more of his beer and thought about it. What Lucius had told him confirmed his feeling. He had been right about Yuri. He *had* to trust someone to get the job done and Cherkassy seemed to fit the bill, if he could only find him! This afternoon already seemed a long time away.

"I'll certainly keep it in mind, Lucius, I owe you one. Does anyone here in the government know who you are?"

"Nope, I'm strictly on my own. I report to a man in the War Department in Washington. My reports for the newspaper go directly to him."

"I can't tell you anything about my mission." Richard said. "But it's nice to know we have a friend and you have two as well. If something should go wrong, if you have to get out in a hurry, I have a way. Keep it in mind."

He stood up and shook hands with Bulloch before going to get his room key. He had to talk to John and give him all this new information. The room was empty, no John. There was a note for him on the table, it was brief.

L came through. Am leaving to see R right now.

From this he deduced that Lenin had arranged for him to see the Tsar that afternoon. By this evening, it would be all arranged. The Tsar and his family would be ready to leave on the 14th of July if nothing went wrong and John's trip was successful. There was nothing to do but wait.

CHAPTER TWELVE

JOHN KESTREL ADJUSTED the satchel more comfortably on his shoulder and leaving the gate and the guards behind him, started up the long driveway to the Catherine Palace. He hadn't believed Trotsky at first.

"I'm to be the mailman?" he asked incredulity in his voice. "But they must know him, know that I'm the wrong person!"

"Of course they will," Trotsky was patient. "Ivan Ippolitov has been delivering there for years, you are Gregor, his son. That's how things are done here."

He explained that in Russia, Ippolitov had a safe government job, if a lowly one. There was a catch however. In times like these, with thousands of wounded men, if the old man became ill and was away for any length of time, he could come back and find his job taken by someone else.

"So finding his son delivering for him will come as no surprise to the guards." Trotsky explained.

"I didn't know the Romanov's were allowed mail."

"They are, but it's censored and only letters or magazines in Russian are allowed."

"Does this man, Ippolitov, see the former Tsar regularily?"

"No. Usually he hands it in at the door, or sometimes he sees Colonel Kobylinsky, but on this occasion we have fixed it. The two men on the door will allow you in to see Romanov. You have a maximum of an hour before the shift changes, but make it less than that, the ones on the gate will wonder what is keeping you."

"I'm very grateful for this chance to beat out the rest of the world." John told him. "Please give my thanks also to Comrade Lenin when you see him."

"Just write a good interview." Trotsky told him. "Make it as positive as you can for us."

"I'll let you see it before I send it." John promised. "I'm sure that you will be pleased."

He was prepared to write that the former Tsar was thinking about joining the Bolshevik Party if it would get him in the door and out again.

John rapped on the door of the Palace and was admitted by one of the guards. He handed him the mail that Ippolitov had provided. The guard looked through it and gave him back two opened letters. John looked at them. The name of the addressee had been crossed out and 'Nicholas Romanov' substituted. He followed the guard across the enormous hallway that Richard had described and climbed a flight of stairs. Thanks to their intensive study of the plans, he knew exactly where he was going. Down a long carpeted hallway to entrance of the suite occupied by the family. The guard knocked premptorily on the door and opened it.

"Keep it short." He told John quietly. "Half an hour and I'll be back for you."

He closed the door behind him and at the end of the room he saw King George getting up from a writing table. The rest of the family were absent. Richard had told him how much the Tsar resembled his cousin, but seeing was another matter. Nicholas moved towards him, his eyes taking in the brassard on his right arm and official cap of the mail service. Nicholas was plainly surprised to see him.

"You have something for me? An official document?"

John handed him the two envelopes he had brought with him and inclined his head.

"Yes, your Majesty, I have brought myself." He spoke in English. "I am John Kestrel, the companion of Captain Cromwell, who saw you earlier. I bring news."

Nicholas Romanov gave him one quizzical look then his bearded face split into an enormous grin and he extended his hand.

"My God! You've actually done it! A thousand welcomes Mr Kestrel. Since the Captain's visit we have lived in a world between hope and despair. Before, we had only ourselves and the good wishes of many Russians, but with his visit we allowed ourselves to hope that something else was being done. Let me call for my wife, she will be overjoyed to see you."

"No Sire, please do not. I don't have much time. I have to tell you that we have come up with a plan to take you out of here. It will happen on the evening of July 14, a few days from now."

Nicholas took a seat on a couch and motioned Kestrel to take one on another facing him. He picked up a cigarette packet from the table between them, took one out and lit it. He took a deep drag on it and exhaled in a long breath, the smoke wreathing about him.

"Tell me what we must do." He asked simply. "How do we leave?"

"Out the front door." John told him.

"On that evening," John continued, "just when it is getting dark, Richard will arrive posing as Yuri Cherkassy again. Colonel Kobylinsky will be expecting him. He will have questions for the entire family and all of you will assemble in the library where you met before. You will not be returning to your rooms. You will be dressed normally, no baggage of any kind. Everything you wish to take must be on your persons. He will speak with you for a few moments. At this point, we can still go back if anything has gone wrong and no one will know anything. Captain Cromwell will leave and you will all enter the secret passage that begins in the library."

"Wait!" Nicholas protested. "I told the captain when he was here that these passages are useless, they are known to all of the guards. It is the first place they will look!"

"Not if they think that you have already left!" John told him smiling.

This was the chink that Richard had seen. The impossibility of getting seven people out without being seen.

"So we let them be seen!" Richard had told John in their room at the Astoria. "I go there and see the family. They enter the passage and the guards inside the house see me leave alone."

"Between the door and the gate is a drive of four minutes. We put together paper mache mannequins resembling some of the family. I prop them up in the front and back seats of the car. In the dark, they will look like people. As I approach the gate, I rev the car and smash through the gate shooting a few shots in the general direction of the guards.

This will create massive confusion and hopefully all the guards will immediately take off after me and the family. The guards inside the house will be at a loss, they didn't see them leave, but will assume that somehow they got outside and got in the car. While they are chasing me around the countryside, you drive through the gate in an ambulance right to the front door. You go inside, get them out of the passage, into the ambulance and drive off in the the opposite direction."

John told all this to a silent Nicholas. His head nodded up and down a few times as he saw the plan unfold. John finished and looked expectantly at the Tsar.

"What do you think, Your Majesty?"

Nicholas stubbed out his cigarette and looked into space, thinking.

"I have a question or two, Mr Kestrel. First, won't they search the house?"

"Yes they will, eventually. We are counting on the confusion of the first ten minutes. The guards at the gate will see you leave, they will *know* that you are gone and take immediate steps to catch you. The guards inside will wonder what is going on but they will *know* that you are still here. Any search made will be perfunctory, to confirm what they already know. Someone will be sent to the house here to inform the guards and with any luck, suspicion will be rife. As you have seen, discipline is not among their qualities."

"All right, I have another question. How many know about this? I regret to say that my Countrymen are not known for keeping secrets."

"At the moment only two, Sire. Captain Cromwell and myself. This will be expanded to three more. I will need help to get you all in the ambulance and Richard will need a driver plus the man who will supply the other two, five in all."

"Last question. After we are free of here, where do we go?"

"Murmansk. A British cruiser will be standing by to take you off. It will arrive on the night of the 15th or early on the 16th. We plan to skirt St Petersburg entirely, meet up with the captain on the other side, change cars and travel as discreetly as possible to Murmansk."

Nicholas leaned back and lit another cigarette. He did some more wall staring then came back to face Kestrel.

"I'm impressed, Mr Kestrel! It is simple and daring. It carries some risk, but then, everything is risky. If we are caught, we are no worse off than we were before. I like it!"

"I beg your pardon, Sire, but that is not correct. If we are caught, you may very well face summary execution. I and the captain, certainly. At the moment, the Petrograd Soviets are quiet, but the news of your attempted escape would fill them with fury.

I feel obliged to tell you this before you make a decision and we're running out of time. The guard should be back for me at any moment."

Nicholas stood up and walked over to the window and stood looking out for a moment before turning back.

"We go, Mr Kestrel, we go! I and my family will be ready on the night of the 14th." He grinned at him. "It's really quite exciting, isn't it? The girls will be thrilled at the prospect." He strode forward to a standing Kestrel and took his hand again. "I thank you again for bringing both hope and excitement into our lives. God speed to you and we'll see you soon."

John went to the door and opened it to find the guard already approaching. He had timed it just right. Back down the corridor, down to the hall and out the door into the sunlight. *'By God, he had done it!'* He started down the driveway only to be halted by the guard's voice.

"You! Ippolitov, stop!"

He turned slowly, sweat suddenly breaking out under his tunic. The guard was standing on the top step of the palace waving at him.

"You forgot to take the letters with you!"

He stared blankly at the guard before realising that the mailman would also carry outgoing mail as well. He went back and sheepishly accepted the mail from the guard, turned and made his way to the gate where the car waited to take him to Tsarkoe Selo train station and the journey back to St Petersburg.

"You got everything you needed?" Trotsky asked him.

John was back in the Smolniy Institute again. Trotsky and Zinoviev were the only two in the small back room. Lenin was still off somewhere.

"Oh yes Comrades, I had a very good interview. Nicholas Romanov was most co-operative. He was most penitent for the acts that he and his family have committed against the people, but he strongly defended his wife against any charges of aiding the Germans. He said it was ridiculous."

Trotsky and Zinoviev exchanged glances.

"That may very well be true, Comrade Redding." Trotsky said, "but you don't have to print that bit, do you? It would upset the people who want to see a true penitent."

"I see what you mean, Comrades. He also said that he was happy to support whatever government was in power and abide with it's decisions. Something to the effect that it was a new world now in Russia and he and his family must find their place in it."

Trotsky smiled sourly at that and gave John a frank glance.

"When we come to power, the Romanov's need have no fear on that score, we will find a suitable place for them."

He opened a drawer in the desk and took out a bottle of vodka and two glasses. He gave one each to John and Zinoviev and poured some vodka into each glass. Trotsky himself, did not drink alcohol. He reached behind him and brought forward a glass of mineral water and lifted it.

"You have done a good day's work, Comrade Redding. We salute you!"

They drank together in the toast and John swallowed the firey drink with ease. He hoped that they had swallowed all the lies he had told them with the same ease. Zinoviev put down his empty glass and smiled at John.

"I will drive you back to the Astoria where you can begin work your article. Don't forget to let us see an advance copy will you?"

John assured them that they would see it first before anyone and they left for the short drive back. He was bursting to tell Richard the news and hoped that he would be there when he arrived.

He went through the revolving door of the Astoria and saw Richard sitting alone in the bar. He stopped at the entrance and waited until Richard lifted his head and saw him standing there. He gave a small nod upwards with his head and went up to their room where Richard shortly joined him.

"I got your note," Richard told him. "I hope that you have had a successful day. Before you tell me about it, I have one or two things to tell you. One of them will really pin your ears back."

In a city in the grip of revolutionary fervor, a city in which knowledge really was power, they were two very knowledgeable men.

CHAPTER THIRTEEN

LUCIUS BULLOCH JOINED THEM as they were having breakfast the next morning. John, sipping his coffee, looked over the rim at Bulloch with new eyes. He thought with amusement of the words that Bruce-Lockhart had told Richard about St Petersburg being a city of spies. Now they could add another nationality to the collection. Richard finished his coffee and rose to go.

"I'm off to talk to Yuri, if I can find him." he said.

Bulloch laid down his cup and looked up at him.

"If you want to know where he is, ask me. I have two locals following him about. He was out of town yesterday, but he's back at his lodgings this morning."

"Really?" Richard said. "How convenient." He turned to go, then turned back. "Tell me, Lucius. How do you know that these two locals don't already work for Yuri?"

He laughed at him and strode out of the restaurant leaving Bulloch looking thoughtful.

"How would you like to make a lot of money?" Richard asked Yuri Cherkassy.

Cherkassy pushed himself back from the table, raised his eyebrows and looked at Richard.

"Why don't you make that moustache permanent?" He said. "It looks quite good on you, or should I say us? What's a lot of money?"

"Five thousand gold sovereigns." Flat, no intonation.

Cherkassy's eyes widened a little at the amount and his lips pursed as the amount rolled around in his head. With that kind of money, he could pay off everyone he owed and still have a lot left over to do anything he wanted.

"Do I have to kill all of the Duma, or will half suffice?"

"Not quite that drastic. I'm planning a little excursion with some friends. It will be quite exciting and I need someone to help with the operation, suggest two other men, and come along for the ride."

"And where would this excursion be going?"

"England."

"England? Why would you need any help? You can come and go as you please."

"I can, but my friends can't, they need some assistance in getting out of Russia."

Cherkassy leaned forward in his chair and his eyes sharpened.

"I think I see. What do you need? False passports? A friendly guard at the frontier? I can probably arrange that. How many friends do you have going with you?"

"I won't need passports and for this, no guard could be bribed. I have seven friends, five women, a man and a boy."

Richard could almost see Cherkassy's brain working as he juggled the numbers and the sexes around. He suddenly straightened up and his jaw dropped.

"My God! You're going for the Tsar!"

Richard nodded at him, saying nothing.

"It can't be done! And if it was, you'd have all of Russia chasing you!"

"It would be a hell of a story, wouldn't it? You'd be both rich and famous, Yuri."

"I could also be infamous and dead!" Cherkassy retorted. "But tell me, assuming that this was possible, how would it be done, when, and how would I get paid?"

"The how I'll keep to myself for the moment, the when also, but shortly, in a few days. As for payment, half now, the rest afterwards."

Actually, he and John had nothing like five thousand sovereigns, but he was confident that either the Gods or Bruce-Lockart would provide.

"The other men, you provide and you pay. It's a one way trip for everyone. Russia will be too hot to hold any of you. I also need your cooperation in arranging another visit to see the Family again. All of them must be together in the library when I, as Cherkassy, arrive to interview them. I also need your help in planning our escape route. We can't go back through Petrograd and I'm going to need a military truck and a car with staff pennants."

Cherkassy laughed, went to the kitchen and poured them both some more tea. He stood looking down at Richard

"You're not a reporter, are you? You're a spy. Pity, I've been looking forward to that interview story. You know, I could get a medal if I turned you in. Is your name really Pringle?"

Richard just shrugged. "What does it matter? You can't prove anything and you would be a lot poorer by the decision. And if anyone checks, there really is a Mr Pringle who is a reporter for the Guardian and is currently in Russia. And judging by the way your masters have treated you, you might not even get the medal!"

Cherkassy sat down and swirled the tea around in his glass. He looked suddenly sad, Richard didn't know if it was false or not.

"I would have to leave Russia, wouldn't I? That's one thing every true Russian hates, the thought that he might never come back again. You might not think it, Peter, but I am a patriotic Russian, no matter how many mistakes it's rulers make, I love my Country. Hold on a minute."

He rummaged about in his desk and brought out a pad of paper and, licking the end of a pencil, said, "All right, I'm in. What do you need and when?"

"The truck and the staff car. They should be waiting in Okhta, outside the city. We'll have to dump our escape transport, it will be too recognisable."

"Why? What are you using?"

"Now I think of it, you can help me there. I was going to steal an ambulance, but you could arrange that as well."

"An ambulance?"

"Why not? It's the perfect escape vehicle. Keep ringing the bell and everyone gets out of the way. Once they get organised, the word will get out, but by then we'll have dumped it. I'll also need two hand guns."

Cherkassy's face changed, grew serious.

"That's another story. It may seem incongruous in a Country at war, but we keep very careful track of small arms. We have enough trouble with our revolutionary friends without arming them."

Richard thought of the missing American shipment and kept a straight face.

"They're only for show. I've no intention of shooting anyone, but I may have to shoot a couple of rounds for effect."

"When do I see the money?"

"I'll be back in two days, bringing the money with me. Have your uniform and the pass ready for me then. Make sure that Colonel Kobylinsky knows that you're coming." He rose to his feet. "I think that's about it for now." He held out his hand. "It's a brave and noble thing you are doing, Yuri. The name of Cherkassy will echo down in Russian history books."

Cherkassy took his hand and grinned at him.

"That's the thing that worries me, will I be a hero or a traitor in those books?"

Richard grinned back at him. "If it's any comfort, one of our early English writers wrote,

'Treason sir, doth never prosper, for if it does, none dare call it treason.'

Arriving back at the Astoria, he plumped himself down beside John and helped himself to one of the tiny cakes that were before him on the table of the restaurant.

"We're all set, John. Yuri agreed to everything, we just have to come up with some more gold sovereigns. I'm going to see if Bruce-Lockart has left for Moscow. I'll call at the Embassy. As Pringle, I would be expected to in any case. I hope they managed to head the real one off."

There came a sudden shouting and the thud of many boots striking the cobblestones.

"What the devil's that?" he asked.

"All hell's broken loose." John told him. "It's been going on all afternoon. We just got news from the front. The Germans have regrouped and are pushing back, there's a hell of a battle going on in Galicia. Graziani just came back from the war front. It looks bad. Someone has to take charge and stop the German advance."

Richard looked through the window and saw a huge crowd of men and women marching past on the way to the Admiralteskaya. Trotsky's banner, 'Peace, Land, Power to the People' was prominently waved above the crowd.

"I told you it was a premature victory." Richard told him. "The German army is extremely tough and resilient. Kerensky had better call up all the reserves and that will put an end to these demonstrations. Hopefully, all this will calm down and we can get our business done in peace and quiet."

CHAPTER FOURTEEN

THE CIVIL DISTURBANCES DIDN'T EASE off the next day, they got worse. The news from Galicia hadn't helped. It was no longer a defeat, it was a rout. Russian armies were reeling back everywhere in confusion. In desperation, Kerensky rushed every reserve soldier he could find to the front, dangerously weakening his position in St Petersburg. Even the former Tsar was allowed to issue a communique exhorting his countrymen to stem the German tide.

The Square in front of the Winter Palace was thronged with a seething, moving tide of men and women who roared and shouted one slogan after another. Speaker after speaker mounted the platform in front of the Alexander Column to demand one thing or another; Peace, War, Bread, Death to the Tsar, the execution of all the General Staff, and so on. Impassioned rhetoric hung like a pall of smoke over the square. The British, French, Italian and American contingents in the city prudently kept out of the way.

"Lenin is in his element." John told Cromwell that morning. "He thinks that this is it! The Bolshevik Party can now take over the government."

He had just returned from the Smolniy Institute where the Party leaders had been in one frantic meeting after another all night. "He's got every man he can find on the streets pushing for Kerensky to resign and a new government to be formed."

They were standing in the foyer of the Astoria watching two employees pushing brooms to clean up the broken glass of the front windows. The last mob to pass had thrown stones at the hotel and intimidated the small crowd of foreigners watching the turmoil from inside.

"This must have been what the French Revolution was like." Richard observed. "A mindless mob crushing anything in it's path that cries for reason and sanity. I can almost hear the shout of, *"A bas les Aristos!"* They won't be happy until the Germans are at the city gates and they can tell each other it was all the landowner's fault."

"Lenin has to be stopped." John told him.

John Kestrel normally had an even temper and a sunny disposition. Even as a policeman walking the beat on the seamer sides of London's streets, he was philosophical about it.

"There's a balance between us and them." He had told a new recruit to the force. "They break the law, we try to catch them. It's a business. They're on one side and we're on the other. Getting angry will only cloud your judgement."

Working undercover with the unions had reinforced this belief. John had become aware of the desperate conditions that so many were working under and the need for some improvement. He also knew those who would take advantage of that desperation to foment more than legitimate protest and offer simple solutions to complex problems.

Lenin and the Bolshevik Party were offering themselves as the panacea to all their ills. Eliminating the ruling class and ending the war would somehow put bread and jam on every table. More to the point, this attempt to overthrow of the Provisional government could mess up their plans to rescue the Tsar. July 14 was just a few days away.

"Lenin has to be stopped." He repeated. "We have to see your friend, Cherkassy. He can get into see Kerensky."

"Why?" Richard asked. "What can he do, or does this have to do with your secret project?"

"Yes. I think I can put a spoke in Lenin's wheel. I can go through David Mandel, but it would be better coming from Kerensky, he has the power of the government behind him. With all this going on, where would Cherkassy be?"

Richard took a moment to think about it. There were only two places. The General Staff could relent and send him back to the front where he might do some good, or Kerensky might have put him back in charge of the Peter and Paul fortress. Holding that was the key to the city if it was properly manned and led.

"Let's go together to Peter and Paul. He's going to find out about you anyway. If he's there, I can get in to see him. What is it that you've been doing?"

Kestrel told him. Richard looked at him in amazement then a grin spread over his face. The grin became a laugh until he roared, to the surprise of other hotel guests. The two sweeping up the glass stopped to see if they were object of the laughter.

"It's priceless! Richard choked on the words between gasps. "I love it! You're quite right, Kerensky is the best person for this, if he has the balls for it. Let's go!"

Alexander Kerensky was a deeply worried man. Five months ago, he and others had been swept into power in a popular and largely bloodless, uprising. The sudden sense of freedom had gone to their heads. There was an indescribable feeling of joy. Of letting sunlight into a long closed and curtained room. They had been determined that the trappings of a dead monarchy would be swept away and new, cleaner government take it's place. That feeling had lasted about three days before all the various groups that had banded together to make the revolution had started squabbling among themselves.

Kerensky fiddled nervously with the letter opener on his desk. He had the long, sensitive fingers of a pianist, which did not match the rest of him. He was a short man, about 5'7" with reddish brown hair that was starting to recede. His dark brown inquisitive eyes were set in a fresh complexioned face which always had a smile handy. After joining the Narodniki party twelve years ago, his natural dynamism and intelligence had pushed him to become the leader five years later. Now he was one of the leaders in the Duma, not that that counted for much. They had been expected to be a rubber stamp for the war cabinet and to endorse and support every disastrous decision of Protopopov and the others.

In March, he had become first, Minister of Justice and later, almost by default, Prime Minister. In that first flush of anger and enthusiasm, when tempers had run high, he'd personally saved three cabinet ministers from assassination. His was the voice of reason crying out among all those howling for blood. Now he was in danger of being thrown off the back of the sled to appease the peace mongers, Plekhanov and Lenin, especially Lenin.

He thought of Vladimir Ilyich Ulyanov as his personal cross to bear. Alexander and Vladi had grown up in Simbirsk on the Volga although Vladi was eleven years older than him. Alex's father, the headmaster of the school, had taught both of them. Vladimir had left for exile in Siberia and he had thought no more about him until arriving in St Petersburg and finding that he had become a hidden power among the various underground societies. Vladimir had split with Plekhanov and the Mensheviks and gone with the Bolsheviks, controlling things from Switzerland.

As leader of the Narodniki, Alexander had tried to hammer out some points of agreement with the other splinter parties, but Vladimir, or Lenin, as he now wanted to be called, had refused to compromise an inch. Since his return in April, he had been a thorn in his side, undermining him at every opportunity.

The Country was a mess and trying to maintain some kind of order and run a war was an impossible job. Thanks to the paranoia of the Tsar's father, the Russian railroad gauge was different from the rest of Europe and the army was equipped to wipe the floor with Napoleon's army, not a modern one.

He would never admit it, but he would also like to get out of the war if he could think of a way to do it with some semblance of honor. He was balanced on a knife edge, tiptoeing along it, trying keep from falling on the blade. As leader of the Country, he needed the recognition of other Countries and he also desperately needed their trade and credit for next winter. The price he had to pay was continuing the war and keeping fifteen German divisions away from the Western Front in Belgium and France.

The rioting and looting in the city had him at his wit's end. He was loath to call out those few remaining troops to quell the disturbances. Firstly, he had a natural aversion to using the same force that he had accused the Tsar of using to do the same thing. And secondly, he wasn't at all sure that the army would obey his commands.

All there was left was the wounded, the malcontents and not a few deserters who had been pardoned in the new situation. The only crack troops he had left were in the Peter and Paul under Cherkassy. Which reminded him, Cherkassy was waiting to see him.

He wondered what he wanted. He had read his record and in spite of everything, he had to like the man. He was a rogue, but a likeable one. He had also read between the lines of the record and made some inquiries. If they had had more like him, they might not be suffering so many defeats. He pushed a number of papers on his desk to one side and rang the little bell. The door opened and Piotr, his secretary, stuck his head in.

"Send in Cherkassy and leave us alone unless the Germans are at the gates offering to surrender."

The door opened again and Yuri Cherkassy, in full uniform, strolled in with that insolent officer's gait that always set his teeth on edge. He thrust the thought aside and gave him his ever ready smile.

"What brings you over from Peter and Paul, Yuri Pavlovich? I hate to say it, but I may have need of you and your men before the day is out. I really don't see any alternative."

Cherkassy sat down in the chair before Kerensky and crossed his legs. He brought out a chased silver cigarette case and lit up, taking his time about it. He blew a cloud of blue smoke into the air.

As to that, Mr Prime Minister, I may have just the solution that you've been looking for." He blew another cloud of smoke and gave Kerensky a knowing smile. "How would you like to get rid of Lenin and the whole Bolshevik Party in one fell swoop?"

CHAPTER FIFTEEN

KERENSKY'S FIRST FEELINGS were of exultation and hope, then reason and caution caught up to him. Cherkassy must have something really nasty, but what would the price be? He did what he had always done, he stalled. He said nothing immediately, but rang his bell for Piotr and ordered tea for them both, allowing himself time to think.

"Would you care to enlighten me, Yuri Stepanovich?"

Cherkassy marvelled at Kerensky's self control. The man was hanging on by his fingertips and he orders tea?

"I have in my possession information that shows that Vladimir Ulyanov is a paid agent of German Reich and by implication, the Bolshevik Party also."

There! He had hit the man right between the eyes with it and Kerensky didn't even blink! He looked at him with one eyebrow raised waiting for more information.

Alexander Kerensky thought '*There is a God in heaven!*' but he let no sign of it show. He was wondering about the price.

Cherkassy reached into his tunic pocket and pulled out a manila envelope which he placed before them on the table. He opened the flap and and let two smaller envelopes slide on to the table. Waiting in the ante room he had rehearsed his story. The real one would never do. He indicated the letters with a languid hand,

"Have a look." he invited. "I think you'll be interested."

Kerensky picked up the first one and looked at the outside first. There was no postmark and no addressee save for the letter "U" printed large in black ink. He pulled out the letter and looked at it. It was a two page, hand written letter in German. The date was February 14, 1917. The printed logo at the top was an address on the Wilhelmstrasse in Berlin. That street, as everyone knew, was the heart of the German administration. He looked at the bottom of the second sheet for a signature but saw only the letter, "L" at the end. He looked up from the letter to Cherkassy.

"Unfortunately, I don't read German. Who's it to? And who is it from?"

Cherkassy reached into his other pocket and drew out some sheets, separated them and put two on the desk.

"This, I swear to you, is a fair translation of the letter. You will see that the letter is addressed to Lenin and the sender is probably Ludendorff, I cannot swear to that, but it's a fair assumption. The, "M" referred to in the letter is probably Reinhard Mannheim, A Colonel in the Abwehr, German Military Intelligence. He is known to have been in Geneva during Christmas of 1916."

Kerensky picked up the translation and read through it, his heart beating a little faster.

Dear U,

Following your demand for some written assurances on our agreement, this letter will have to serve. You must keep this in a very safe place and burn it should it's discovery become possible.

We agree to provide you and your entourage with a train to transport you through Germany. This train will be sealed and no one may get off before arriving at our northern frontier. All necessary provisions will be on board. We should have everything ready by late March. M will be in touch with you. From that point, you will be on your own to reach St Petersburg. You have assured us that this will be no problem.

We have established an account in the Royal Bank of Copenhagen in the amount of one million marks under the name you chose. This can only be drawn upon by being co-signed by M. One half of the money will be made available upon your party becoming the government of Russia and the other half .when an armistice or treaty of peace is signed between our two Countries.

Kerensky looked again at the enigmatic, "L" at the bottom of the letter.

"Ludendorff never signed this." he told Cherkassy. "The man is not a fool, he's a soldier and a gentleman, even if he's on the other side."

Cherkassy gave an elaborate shrug. "What do we care who signed it? It will be taken that he did, and that's enough."

Kerensky tapped at the letter with his fingernail.

"This isn't enough, Yuri Stepanovich. Oh, it's damaging, but it's also ambiguous. Lenin will say that it's not him who's referred to."

"Ambiguous?" Cherkassy was irate. "Ambiguous? Do you know any other Russian revolutionary whose name begins with U and who was transported across Germany to arrive here six weeks after the letter was written?"

Kerensky had to admit to that. Lenin had not exactly boasted about it, but it was known that the Germans had done it for their own reasons. It was the second part about the money that was damaging. It would finish him.

"Lenin will say that it's a forgery. That no such letter was ever in his possession. By the way, how did you get it? I must have some provenance."

"Lenin will never miss the letter." Cherkassy told him with an extremely fine degree of truth. "This isn't his letter, it's a copy from Ludendorff's files."

"What! My God, Cherkassy, you're a genius! What did you do, drop in for tea in the Wilhelmstrasse?"

"Sarcasm does not become you, Mr Prime Minister." Cherkassy told him with a touch of asperity. "It came to me by an extremely roundabout road. I know only part of the story, the part that can be verified."

"Please go on Yuri Stepanovich, I'm all ears."

"Ludendorff lives in a house in the Wannsee, a posh part of Berlin. Five weeks ago, his house caught on fire. It wasn't destroyed, but there was damage. This was reported in the Berlin papers, I have seen a copy. The servants who live there were ordered to the study where they literally threw boxes and drawers full of papers through the window of the study to the lawn outside.

The fire department arrived and the house was saved. The boxes and drawers were gathered up to be restored to a safe place. A servant engaged in this task, hid several papers on his person at the time. This same servant was almost immediately discharged when it was found that it was his carelessness that had started the fire"

Kerensky started to smile, seeing where this was going.

"My own feeling is that he knew what was coming and took advantage of the situation to grab anything that might be worth something. What other papers he may have taken, I have no idea, but these two ended up in the hands of a cousin of mine who lives in Riga and he brought them to me when Riga was evacuated by our forces."

"You said two papers, can I assume that this other letter is also as damaging?"

"Not quite, but it supplements the other. I assume that both were together in the same file. But see for yourself."

Kerensky pulled out the second letter from it's envelope. It was only half of a letter, the top half had been destroyed by burning. The edge of the remaining piece was charred and blurred. What was left was also in German and Kerensky looked expectantly at Cherkassy who pulled the remaining translation from his pocket and handed it over.

'-ratulated, Mannheim. When we have news of U's arrival in St Petersburg, you will make your way to Copenhagen and wait there for further instructions. You will disburse no money without my written authority. While there, you will also call upon the German—'

There, the letter ended. He looked up at Cherkassy.

"I think that there probably was a second page to the letter." Cherkassy told him. "It was lost or burned. It doesn't matter, the important part is there. The paymaster is being ordered to Copenhagen to pay out to Lenin when instructed. I think it's pretty dammning, don't you?"

Alexander Kerensky put the letter and it's translation back into the envelope and turned away from Cherkassy to look out of the window, his mind churning. He didn't know if the letters were forgeries or not, and right at the moment, he couldn't afford to care. They were dynamite! He turned back.

"You are to be congratulated in exposing this viper's nest in our bosom! I owe you my heartfelt thanks. Why don't you go back to the fortress, pick out some men and run round to the Smolniy and arrest Lenin and as many others as you can lay your hands on."

"With respect sir, that may be a mistake. An arrest without any apparent reason would only inflame the people. Why not see that these letters are first printed in this evening's paper? Along with suitable commentary. Then, when I go around to arrest him, I might actually be helped by the people. The citizens of Petrograd are afraid and angry, but they are loyal Russians!

Kerensky smiled at him. "My dear Cherkassy, you are quite right! The paper comes out at five, doesn't it? Why not wait until six, then go and arrest them. Clap them in the fortress and we'll think of proper charges to make in the morning."

Yuri smiled conspiritorially and rose to go, but was waved down again by Kerensky's hand.

"It occurs to me, Yuri Stepanovich, that we have not been making proper use of your talents. I have read your file and I know that you were badly treated. Perhaps now is the time to make up for that. Can you suggest anywhere that might be a better position? Back in the army perhaps?"

Kerensky needed all the allies that he could get and this wily ex-officer might be just the man he needed to get things done. Yuri Cherkassy settled back in his chair and his mind ran quickly over his prepared speech.

"Well," he began, "there are one or two things you should be aware of."

At seven that evening, Cherkassy phoned Kerensky.

"I have a dozen people locked up in the fortress, Mr Prime Minister. Unfortunately, Lenin is not among them. He's either hiding in the city or has fled to Finland. He was warned, or maybe just lucky. I have the rest of the committee including Trotsky. I have asked for a special watch be put on the border for Lenin, but I doubt that we'll catch him."

"No matter," Kerensky told him cheerfully. "The Bolshevik power has been checked, at least for the moment. Come and see me in the morning and we'll discuss what to do with them."

Yuri Cherkassy hung up the phone in a cheerful frame of mind. The English spies' plan had succeeded brilliantly. It had been decided to let Yuri take all the credit for it, which was all right with him. Kerensky was happy, the English were happy, only Vladimir Ulyanov was the loser, whch was only as it should be. He lifted the phone again. He had a couple of important calls to make, tomorrow was the 14th of July.

In a farmhouse outside of Helsinki, Lenin nursed his anger and looked for someone to blame. It had been luck that he had been in Mathilde Kashinskaya's house when the printer from the newspaper called to warn him of the article coming out. He had tried to call the Smolniy to warn them, but the line had been busy. He had been so close!

"Feliks, I want you to find out who did this to us, then we'll extract vengeance."

Feliks Dzerzhinski, his chief of security and all around hatchet man, was a tall, cadaverous man with deep set eyes and a graying beard. He had also been at the ballet star's home when the news came and they had gone together. He nodded to Lenin.

"It couldn't have been Kerensky." Feliks told him. "He's not smart enough to have thought it up. It had to have been someone else who did it and gave it to him."

Vladimir Ulyanov brooded in the light from the fire. Who could have done it? It was a blatant forgery. He would never be so stupid as to hold anything like that in writing. Besides, they were wrong. The money was in Basel, not Copenhagen.

Richard Cromwell toasted John Kestrel with his glass.

"A brilliant coup, my friend! Our main opponent is out of the way and his supporters are in disarray. Yuri should now be in solid with Kerensky which won't do us any harm. Tomorrow is Bastille Day. Let us hope that we can successfully storm our Bastille and rescue our prisoners."

John raised his own glass in reply. By late tomorrow night, they should be on their way with the family or being measured for two holes in the ground. He hoped it was the former.

CHAPTER SIXTEEN

JULY 14 DAWNED BRIGHT and sunny, promising to be a real scorcher. After breakfast, Cromwell and Kestrel went across the Neva to Vasilevskiy Island to an address Cherkassy had given them. They met him behind the Lutheran church just off of Bolshoy Prospekt. This part of town had been heavily German until the beginning of the war and now many houses and factories were vacant. He led them to a lock up and pushed open the large double doors. The sun streamed into the dusty interior.

"Have a look." he invited.

There were two vehicles standing in the middle of the floor. One was a dun colored ambulance with a large red cross painted on each side. Above the cab was a brass bell with a cord stretching into the cab to warn traffic to stay clear. The other was a brand new monster 220K Mercedes touring car.

"Jesus!" Richard exclaimed in admiration, turning to Cherkassy. "Where did you get it?"

"Spoils of war." Yuri told him. "It was impounded when the German Ambassador left. Protopopov got it when he became Minister of War and we got it when we threw him out. It ah, fell into my hands for safe keeping so to speak." He grinned at Richard. "It should be big enough for you. Try not to get any holes in it, I'd like it back in one piece."

He handed over the authorization papers and gravely took the money belt that Richard handed over to him which contained almost all their gold sovereigns.

"It won't be dark until nine to night." Yuri reminded him. "I told the colonel that duties prevented me getting there before eight-thirty. He will have the family waiting for you in the library. I will meet you in Tsarskoe Selo at eight tonight with the two men I found for you. They don't know what they're doing, but I've paid them enough not to ask questions. I have a truck and a staff car waiting in Okhta for the transfer. I will also be there to get back my beautiful Mercedes."

"You'll have to leave it, Yuri. That car will stand out like a sore thumb. It can probably outrun anything in the Country, but it can't outrun a roadblock."

Cherkassy looked at the car with sadness. "Is there anything else?"

"Not that I can think of, Yuri. John and I have to go and get the dummies and bring them here and we're all set."

After some experimenting, they had found that using papier mache was too difficult, a substitute was found.

Two nights ago, he and John had broken in to one of Petrograd's largest department stores and stolen four mannequins and the clothing to go with them. They had taken them from the storeroom and hopefully, their absence would not be noticed until later. The safe house held them until they knew where the car would be.

Cherkassy opened his jacket and buckled the money belt about his waist. He refastened his jacket, patted it with a smile and waved adieu to them both.

"Until tonight, then."

John slammed the back door of the ambulance where he had been examining the inside. He stood beside Richard as the lockup door slammed shut.

I've checked both cars, they're fueled up and ready to go. Are you sure that you can trust him?"

His policeman's antipathy to villains coming up.

"We don't have a hell of a lot of choice, John. At some point we had to burn our bridges with someone, and he seems like our best bet. Let's take the ambulance to get the dummies, we can see how it drives."

The huge Mercedes growled to a stop in front of the gates leading to the royal residences. The driver, Ivan, put on the brake and looked at Cromwell. They had decided to call both of Cherkassy's drivers Ivan, it was easier than learning their real names, and safer. It was almost full dark as Richard held out the pass to one of the gate guards who held up his lantern to see him more clearly.

"Comrade Cherkassy? Yes, you are expected."

He waved to the other guard who pushed open the gate to let the car pass. There were five other guards visible at the small guardhouse as he passed through.

The one thing he hadn't been able to check was the strength of the gates. They looked more for show than a serious attempt to keep people out. The weight and the speed of the car should prove sufficient on his return trip. The drive wound through the park and they passed the Alexander Palace. "Slow down." he ordered the driver. He was timing it to allow for the halt on the return. The car drew up in front of the Catherine Palace and he got out.

"Turn the car around and be ready to go in ten minutes." He muttered as he got out.

The door was opened for him and the two guards inside snapped to attention as he entered. Their boots shone and their faces were clean shaven. His visit had produced a result. Richard didn't think he liked that, he preferred them sloppy and unable to deal with what was coming up. He was ecorted to the library door and he stepped through for his first sight of the entire family.

Cromwell's eyes raked the room and saw first the Tsar standing by the fireplace and second, in the foreground, Colonel Kobylinsky who came towards him.

"I hope that this is important, Cherkassy" Kobylinsky growled at him. "I realize that the Committee works long hours, but it's almost nine in the evening. Will you be long?"

"Not long at all, Colonel, a few minutes only." he replied easily, hiding his tension. "There's a meeting tomorrow morning at the Tauride Palace and some questions will be raised about the family and Mr Kerensky wanted to be ready with the answers. Would you introduce me before you leave?" This was a calculated piece of insolence, but he had to have the Colonel out of the room. Kobylinsky raised an eyebrow and smiled slightly. "Certainly."

He bowed over Alexandra's hand and brushed his lips lightly to it. She was a tall woman, not very pretty and with her hair done up on ther top of her head. To his eye she seemed to be dripping with jewellry. The girls were gravely proper and each gave a small curstey as he bowed before them. Alexis didn't get up from the couch he was lying on. He seeemd pale and tired as Cromwell gave him a short bow. He hoped he could walk the few yards necessary. Nicholas came forward from his place at the empty fireplace and took his hand.

"Delighted to see you again, Cherkassy. I so enjoyed our last visit. I'm sorry to hear that you don't have much time, we were looking forward to hear you speak of current events. We get few visitors here."

Richard thought that the Tsar was doing just great. He was giving him an option for more time if he needed it.

"I'll see what I can do, Citizen." he replied and glanced at Kobylinsky. That officer took his cue and made his farewells saying that he would be in his office upstairs should he be needed. The door closed behind him and Richard turned to face the family.

There was a collective sigh and Nicholas came forward.

"Captain Cromwell? It is you, isn't it?" the Tsar asked in English.

"Yes, Your Majesty. Are you all ready? Is there any problem that I should know about?"

Alexandra came forward again and took his hand with a warm smile on her face.

"We are ready, Captain." She spoke in Russian. "You have no idea what your visits have meant to us. When your fellow companion gave us the details, we were ecstatic! It brought a breath of life and hope to us." She glanced behind at the four girls sitting demurely on the two sofas.

"I think that all of my girls entertain romantic notions about you. You are a knight come to rescue us."

"The most dangerous part has yet to come, Maam." He looked at the Tsar.

"Would you escort your family into the passage, Sire? It should not be a long wait, perhaps fifteen minutes before my comrade comes to get you out. He will have an ambulance waiting outside, please be as quick as possible when he comes."

The Tsar moved to a bookcase beside the fireplace and pressed on the end. The whole bookcase moved out from the wall revealing a gaping dark entrance. He reached inside and removed a lantern from a hook on the passage wall and lit it. He went first to Alexis and lifting him, moved into the tunnel. The girls followed, then Alexandra. Nicholas appeared once more at the entrance to swing it shut. He glanced at Richard and grinned at him.

"L'audace, mon Capitaine, toujours, l'audace."

He closed the passage door and Richard was left alone in the room.

Richard decided to give it another five minutes before leaving to give the appearance of reality. He allowed himself one cigarette then strode to the door, took a deep breath and went through.

A guard in the hall straightened up and looked at him. Richard paused at the door, looked back and spoke to the empty room.

"Thank you, you have been most helpful."

He walked purposefully to the door which the guard opened for him. Standing on the steps, he looked for the car observing that it was now full dark.

The twin headlights of the Mercedes crept forward and Ivan jumped out to open the door for him. They swept down the drive at speed and entered the first curve hiding them from view of the house. The car stopped, they jumped out and went back to the boot. He and Ivan carefully lifted out the dummies and placed them in prominent view on the back seat. Two facing forward and two facing back. Richard adjusted the hats the dummies were wearing to cover the waxy faces and they jumped back in the front of the car. Ivan released the hand brake and looked at him. Richard took the guns out of each pocket and gave one to Ivan.

"When we hit the gate, start shooting, but for God's sake, don't hit anyone! We just want to start a chase, not a war."

The massive engine growled to life, they drove past the moon silvered pond and past the last stand of trees before the gatehouse. Peering through the windshield he could see that the gatehouse was lit up and also that the gates had a light suspended over it. There was also one other thing, the gates were open! It was a marvellous stroke of luck. The guards must have been thinking about his return and left them open to save time. Richard gave Ivan a swift look.

"Put your foot to the floor, but slow down just enough at the gate for them to see us."

The car leapt to life and they hurtled down the driveway towards the gate. The two guards saw them coming and startled, started to unsling their rifles. Ivan put his hand on the horn, the sound blasting into the quiet air. As the car arrived at the gate, Richard could see three more men boiling out of the guardhouse door. He leant out of the window and snapped off three quick shots in their general direction.

Three guards dived for the ground as they swept through the open gates. He looked back and ducked as one of the prone guards managed to get off a shot. They hurtled down the tree lined road until they approached a curve. He told Ivan to slow down and stop before the curve.

"We want them to chase us, give them some time."

He kept his eyes glued to the light from the gate about five hundred yards away. Ivan had the car in neutral with his foot tapping nervously on the pedal. "Wait for it, Ivan, wait for my signal."

He saw headlights spring to life and a car emerged from the gates, turning in their direction. "Go!" he snapped. The gears engaged and the car drifted round the corner into the next straightaway. Turning back to face front, Richard saw the headlights of three trucks glaring at him, completely blocking the road. By the lights of his own car he could see a squad of armed soldiers on either side of the trucks, their rifles pointed in his direction.

The Mercedes slowed down to stop just before the road block and Richard turned to his companion to find that he was also looking at a revolver pointing in his direction. The gun that he had given him!

"Please get out of the car, Mr Pringle, there is no- where to run."

Ivan's voice had changed. He was no longer a simple, uneducated soldier. There was an echo of command in the tone. Richard fumbled for the door handle, a lot of thoughts flashing through his head at the same time. Blinded by the healights, he stood with his hands in the air. The gun was taken and the dummies were hauled out of the car to be thrown by the wayside. Ivan motioned him with the gun to get in the back of the Mercedes and joined him there. One of the soldiers climbed in the front and reversed the car in a three pointer until it was heading back to the estate.

The car pulled to a halt in front of the Catherine Palace and he was motioned out. There was also an ambulance parked in front with the motor running. John must have made it inside before the trap was sprung. He was hustled through the hall and into the library that he had left only a short time before.

His eyes went to the bookcase/door, it was open and gaping empty. John was sitting on a sofa in his ambulance attendant uniform. His eyes came up as Richard entered and he shrugged. Against the wall with a gun held by his side was the other Ivan, John's driver. Standing by the fireplace, looking at him, was Yuri Cherkassy.

Richard had been expecting it, but it was still a small shock. Yuri was the only one who could have betrayed them. He wondered if he would learn why before they were shot.

CHAPTER SEVENTEEN

CHERKASSY LOOKED AT THE GUARD who had entered behind Richard.

"Has he been searched?"

"Yes, Comrade Colonel."

Richard noted the title and the promotion, but said nothing. Yuri sighed at the guard.

"Do it again."

This time, they found the knife strapped to his leg and the guard, with some embarrassment, put it down on the table and left. Cherkassy moved from his position at the fireplace, holding a long barreled German Mauser pistol negligently in his right hand. He told the other guard that he could go and motioned to Richard to sit on the sofa with John. Yuri sat down on a chair opposite the sofa and placed the gun on the table between them, but not close enough for a grab.

"Well, here we are again Peter, or whatever your name is"

Richard just looked at him. There didn't seem to be much to say. Cherkassy put his hand in his pocket and produced a photo which he skimmed across the table to him.

"Have a look." He invited.

Richard picked it up. It was a photo of a man taken from fifty feet away. He was in a shed of some kind, then he recognized the place. It was the customs shed at Murmansk. The man was opening a bag for inspection in front of an officer.

"Do you know who he is?" Cherkassy asked. Richard threw the photo back to him.

"I've no idea, should I?"

"You should, it's you. Or rather, it's Mr Peter Pringle clearing customs at Murmansk yesterday. Funny thing about that, he went through into the main area for the trains and was stopped by a man. We don't know what was said, but Mr Pringle immediately turned around and got back on board the ship!" He smiled at him. "Would you like to tell me your real name?"

Richard thought about it. It didn't really matter any more.

"My name is Richard Cromwell, Captain in the British Army."

Yuri's gaze switched to John. "How about you?"

"John Kestrel, Detective Sergeant, London Metropolitan Police."

Cherkassy nodded gravely at both of them as if in thanks. He reached out and pulled the gun a little closer to him. Richard had no doubt that he would use it.

"You came close, Peter, I mean Richard. And I came close to really helping you. I was going to do it until you solved my problem for me."

He brought out his cigarette case and passed one across to Richard, John declined. He slid a box of matches across the table and wagged his finger at Richard.

"Please don't do anything with the matches, it would be a shame to spoil everything." He lit his own cigarette and leaned back a little in the chair. "In case you're wondering, the family is safely back upstairs. Kobylinsky and I brought them out as soon as you left."

"What problem did we solve for you?" John asked. "Why did you let us go through with this charade?"

"I wanted to make a point to Kerensky, to convince him that the family must be moved. He's been dithering on it for weeks. I told him about the escape attempt and persuaded him to let it run as a kind of live exercise, if you know what I mean. I confess that I did change the guards. I put my own men in place of the incompetents that were here, just to make sure."

"I really thought you were with us, Yuri." Richard told him. "I believed you in your flat that morning."

"Because I told you the truth, Richard. I was going along with you. But I also told you something else. I am a Russian, with all that implies. The Tsar had to go, but I didn't want him or the family made into martyrs, and your plan made sense, until you very kindly took care of the Bolsheviks for us.

With them out of the way, Kerensky can go ahead and move the family away, somewhere far away where they can be forgotten." He smiled and shook his head at John. "It was brilliant, Mr Kestrel! I doubt that he can ever prove that the letters are forgeries and some mud will always stick to him."

"And what did you get out of it?" Richard asked.

He was feeling tired now. He had gotten his explanation, now all that remained was a convenient wall and two blindfolds. The price of failure was high, but he accepted it. There was no way out of this place, Cherkassy's men surrounded it. He had only one favour to ask and he thought it would be given.

"What did I get out of it?" Cherkassy echoed. "A number of things. I have crept into favor with the Chief Minister of the Country and I am restored to the army with a suitable promotion. Kerensky wanted to make me a General, but I persuaded him that was going too far. You got me out of debt and I got my beautiful Mercedes back!"

He stood and picked up the gun. Richard stiffened, *'Was it to be now? Here?'*

"I have one favour to ask, Yuri. Will you allow me to write a letter? To my father? If it is delivered to Ambassador Buchanan at the embassy, it will reach him. I also ask that John be given the same privilege. It's not too much to ask, is it? "

They both stood up, John wondering if he had time to reach the small knife strapped to his forearm, it had been overlooked in the cursory search they had made of him.

"Letters?" Cherkassy laughed at them and holstered the gun. "Letters? You can write as many as you like, from England! I'm not going to shoot you, I'm sending you home! You have done the State some service and it will be rewarded. As we have been speaking, your belongings were being taken out of my Mercedes and transferred to the car I drove here. It's waiting for you outside. Go to Helsinki or Murmansk, the ship is still there." His smile stopped. "But don't show your face in Petrograd again. I won't be so generous next time."

Things around Richard suddenly took on a clarity that he'd never experienced. The pattern on the rug leapt out at him in detail. He could see every book in the false bookcase. He could count each individual freckle on John's face. They were going to live!

Yuri Cherkassy smiled at them, went to the library door, opened it and waved them through. The two Ivans were waiting outside and escorted them to the front door of the Palace and closed the door behind them. They stood on the steps in the warm evening air and just breathed for a moment before descending to the waiting car.

The headlights of the car slashed a path through the darkness as John drove them in the direction of Petrograd. They hadn't said much to each other, it was still sinking in. They had come to Russia on a desperate venture and had almost succeeded and now they were going home, not exactly in disgrace, but without any laurels on their brows.

The car topped a rise and they could see the lights of Petrograd before them. John slowed down and pulled off the road. He cut the motor and turned to Richard.

"We've just been run out of town!" he told him.

Richard smiled and nodded in the darkness.

"It does look like that, but at least we're alive to talk about it."

"I don't like it, it offends me."

"Perhaps, but there's not much we can do about it. By tomorrow, our descriptions will be circulated all over town. Yuri meant what he said, if he sees us again he really will have us shot. Our mission has failed, there's no way we can get in again. There's nothing we can do but go home."

"There is one thing that Cherkassy doesn't know." John said slowly. "He doesn't know that we have an apartment in Petrograd under different identities. We could go to ground, change our appearance and try something else."

"There's something else he doesn't know." Richard added. "He doesn't know that there's an American agent in town looking for a lot of guns and looking at him as chief suspect."

"Why don't we drive to the flat and think about it." John suggested. "If we can't think of anything, we can still leave town in the morning."

He started the car and they continued through the night towards the beckoning lights of St Petersburg.

CHAPTER EIGHTEEN

KEEPING ONE HAND ON THE THROTTLE, John Kestrel looked backward out of the cab and backed up just a little. There was a clang as the buffers met. Satisfied, John climbed down out of the cab and strolled back to uncouple the engine from it's load.

Dawn was just breaking and the lights in the marshalling yard were dimming. John had got the job last week at the Finland station in Petrograd. It was the main station to Moscow and all points East. With so many men away, they had been anxious to have him but, like any other new man, he was given the worst shift; eight at night to eight in the morning, but it suited him just fine.

With the war, the station and the yard were busy all night. John was kept fully occupied making up trains and unloading them. Troop trains, freight trains, guns to the front, wounded coming back from it. His experience in the yards of the LMS in London had stood him in good stead. He wouldn't like to try and drive an engine all the way to Moscow, but he could shunt wagons around and it gave him an opportunity to explore the area without being noticed and keep his ears and eyes open.

John and Richard had hammered it out that night in the apartment. The night they had returned from their expulsion from Catherine Palace. The night they had failed in their escape attempt. The night they had been thrown out of town.

"We have to have some kind of plan." Richard had said.

"We can't just sit here and twiddle our thumbs."

John went down on his knees and pulled out from under the bed, one of the suitcases he had previously transferred to the safe house. He opened it and pulled out a bottle of Highland Mist whiskey.

"Remember I brought all these for bribery and corruption purposes? I think we deserve one drink apiece, it will help us ponder our next move."

They sat in silence for twenty minutes, sipping the whiskey, each thinking their thoughts. Both of them pulled in different ways. To go home to relative safety or stay on the job. John put the cap back on the bottle and returned it to the suitcase

"I was thinking about something you told me." John began. "Do you remember telling me about Arras and the offensive? How it was supposed to be a big secret, but everyone down to the camp dog knew about it?"

"These things don't happen in a vacuum," Richard replied. "Anyone with half an eye could see the preparations being made. The ammunition, shells and ambulances that appeared. The object was to keep it a secret from the Germans."

"Just the point that I was going to make. Cherkassy told us that the Tsar and his family are going to be sent far away, when and where we don't know. Far away from here is East or South. That means the Urals or the Black Sea and the only way you can get there from here is by train."

"So how does that help us?"

"It goes with what you just said, *'these things don't happen in a vacuum.'* Kerensky can't decide on a Tuesday that everyone goes on Wednesday. There are preparations to be made. Guards to be chosen, food to be ordered, a train to be made up."

Someone, somewhere has to issue orders to make up a train for a long journey. I've worked in the railroad yards. If I'm close to the scene, I can perhaps find out when and where they're going."

"Assuming that you do find this out," Richard said slowly, "how does it help us?"

"I haven't the faintest idea!" John laughed at him. "But it's better than going back to England with our tails between our legs. The very least we can do is gather information on what is going on here. The Grenville will return again on August 14. Let's give it a month to see if we can come up with something then we can return and give the Admiral an up to date picture of the scene here."

"I'll need you to go a theatrical supply store and get me some things." Richard said, enthusiasm creeping into his voice. "If I let my beard grow and dye it, it will help. I'll try and keep an eye on Cherkassy and develop some contacts." He eyed the suitcase. "Spread some of that largesse around. We also have to get in touch with Bruce-Lockhart somehow, advise him of the situation and get some more money."

John spent wisely in the theatrical supply store. Buying the best kit available and supplementary props, uniforms and clothing to suit any eventuality. In a country at war and a city in the grip of a revolution, it was easy to slip between the cracks in the administration.

John climbed back into the cab and patted the throttle handle affectionately. The engine had been built in Birmingham in 1890 and had seen good service. He looked through the front window at the green light and lifted his hand to the whistle to signal the yard master and paused.

There were dozens of sidings all around him where rolling stock was parked until it's priority was decided and a train made up. A sliding door had just opened on a car two sidings over from him. A man climbed down and closed the door, locking the padlock. John strained to make him out in the gray morning light. The man turned from the door and walking away, went through one of the overhead lights. It was Yuri Cherkassy! John made a careful note of the car and pulled the whistle to resume his shunting. His shift was almost over.

It was full daylight when John returned to the car. He looked, but no one was paying any attention. To be sure, he banged on the door twice, no answer. From his pocket, he took the little kit he had brought with him from London. It would give him entree through most doors. In a moment he had the door open and climbed inside.

The car was three quarters empty, the remaining space being taken up by wooden crates stacked in rows of threes.

One stack had been made into a desk with a folding chair in front of it. John moved further into the car and looked on the makeshift desk for any paperwork, none. The crates were all stencilled, THIS SIDE UP, at one end and, MEDICAL SUPPLIES, at the other.

John knew that this was garbage. He had just spent all night making up a train filled with medical supplies, which were in desperate need at the fluid front where the Russian army was still trying to stem the German tide. On top of one case was a clawhammer. He picked it up and went to a stack at the back out of the way. He had just inserted the claw into one crate when he heard the door of the car slam open.

He cursed himself for a fool. The folding chair meant that someone was on guard here! He turned from the case, the hammer held casually in his hand and moved back a few steps to see a dark haired, broad shouldered man looking at him in surprise. He waved at him with his free hand and smiled.

"So, they've got you on this too? Old Vladi's going crazy back there. He's lost an entire car of medical supplies. I was just going off shift when he told me to start looking." He gestured with his hand. "Looks like I found some of them. Want to give me a hand to open one? We might as well make sure."

He turned his back to the man, his every sense alerted. If this man was a genuine railroad employee he expected some reply, some question, but he didn't think he would get any.

He heard the slither of feet across the floor and spun quickly around, his hand with the hammer extended. John's hand came down in a sweeping motion, the haft of the hammer diverting the knife that had been meant for his back. The knife, the hand and the man behind it went past him in a kind of paso doble.

John was now at right angles to him. His free hand now came down on the man's wrist and he went with him, swinging the hammer back in a reverse thrust that ended with the hammerhead hitting his assailant in the stomach. The man's breath came out of him with a whoosh and John helped things along by sweeping his legs out from him. John let him go as he fell and then he got a surprise, the man didn't fall, he rolled!

The man made a complete forward roll and came to his feet, the knife still gleaming in his hand. John made a quick upward revision. This was no casual guard or bully boy, this was a trained man, probably a soldier. He sidled back a bit wondering if he should drop the hammer and go for his knife, sheathed on his arm under his shirt. He didn't get the chance, the man leapt forward, the knife slashing in front of him. He leant to one side, parrying the knife again and tried for a kick to the knee. He missed the knee but got his thigh and the man fell back with a grunt.

John watched the eyes and the knife hand and almost missed it when the man changed hands and brought the knife in with a low thrust that scraped along his ribs. He let the hammer go and brought both hands down on the knife wrist, turning the knife back against the holder.

He was conscious of a sharp pain in his side which he ignored for the moment. The knife clattered to the floor of the car and the man again rolled free and came to his feet. They were both panting from their exertions. The man glanced quickly at the knife on the floor and his eyes widened slightly as he saw John reach under his shirt sleeve and produce his own knife, a short, flat, razor sharp, throwing knife that he allowed to slide into his right palm.

John faced his unarmed opponent and balanced himself, ready to move forward. The guard, thinking that discretion was the better part of valor, turned and made a dash for the open door to summon reinforcements.

In a second he was five yards away from John and poised at the door to jump down. The point of the throwing knife entered his back and drove on into a lung. He groaned and pitched forward on to the tracks in full view of anyone who might come along.

John clambered down to the track and pulled the knife out of the man's back. He checked for a pulse and found none, he must have nicked something vital. A look all around, no one in sight yet. He picked up the body and heaved it back into the car then himself, shutting the sliding door after him. He slid down the car wall to the floor and sat with his back against it, allowing reaction to set in. He looked at his hands, they were trembling.

His gaze lifted and he looked at the stranger lying on the floor of the car, he was still dead. As a beat copper in London, he had been in the occasional dust up, even knives once, but he had never killed anyone. It had all happened so fast that he had had no time to think, only react.

John told himself that he had had no choice, the guard had definitely been going to kill him, without even knowing who he was! The guard had thought him a railway worker who had been in the wrong place and had attacked instantly. John decided not to feel too guilty about it.

His attention went back down the car to the stacked crates. That had been what this was all about. Getting painfully to his feet, he discovered what his body had been shouting about in the background. There was blood dripping from the wound in his side. Pulling up his shirt, he looked at it. It wasn't too bad, just a scratch, but he couldn't leave here like this. John went over to the dead man and cut the lining out of his jacket and used it pack the wound and tied the rest around his waist as a makeshift bandage.

John searched around the car until he found the hammer and went back to original task, to open one of the crates. He pried it open carefully, laying the nails to one side and pulled back the waterproof covering and saw just what he had expected. After removing a couple of items, he nailed the crate shut again and turned back to his next problem, what to do with the body? He couldn't leave it there. The man had to have a relief guard coming at sometime.

A disappearance might be glossed over, but not a knifed body. He couldn't cart him away over his shoulder, it was getting busy out there. He had to get out of here and tell Richard what he had found, but first he had to do something with the body!

CHAPTER NINETEEN

LUCIUS BULLOCH GOT OFF THE TRAM at Nevsky and Dumskaya Ulitsa. Another day and no further forward. He had written to be recalled, but had received no answer. He had found out some things, but could go no further without some kind of official sanction, it was frustrating.

There was an outdoor café on the corner and the thought of a cool lemonade propelled him in that direction. He was bumped into by a burly worker in a peasant smock.

"A thousand pardons, comrade." The worker said. "I wasn't looking where I was going."

At the same time, he felt a scrap of paper being pushed into his hand. Bulloch smiled at him and went the few steps to the café, his hand casually in his pocket. Sitting down, he ordered lemonade, reaching over to the next table for a discarded newspaper. When the paper was folded properly in front of his face, he brought out the scrap he had been given and placed it on the paper holding it in place by his thumb.

"Go to Korchnoi Park and watch the chess players." The message read in English. *"Lose your followers first."* Bulloch turned the page and at the same time, slipped the message back into his pocket. He sipped at the lemonade when it came and considered his next action. Finishing, he went over to the tram stop.

The Nevsky Prospekt had several tram lines on it going in different directions further down the line. Bulloch waited until a tram arrived, ignored it until it started off, then jumped on quickly, paid his fare and turned to look out behind him. A cloth capped worker waiting at the stop looked frustrated and had started to run after the tram. Bulloch turned his back on him, satisfied.

Two stops later he caught a tram going back in the opposite direction, passing Dumskaya where he had got on. Half-an-hour, and after two more changes, he arrived at the park and made his way to the chess pavilion.

There were numerous tables set up in the half covered area. The chess boards were painted on to the tables and the players brought their own sets with them. There was always a good crowd there watching the players or waiting their turn to play. He moved casually from one small bunch of spectators to the next, keeping his eyes open and waiting. A voice spoke to him in English behind his back.

"Don't look round, Lucius, I think you're clean, but we'll make sure. I'm putting another address in your pocket, go there. It's on Vasilevskiy Island and make damn sure your not followed!"

He recognised the voice, but gave no sign and allowed a few minutes to pass before moving away from the chess players and looking at the new address. It was a street off of Bolshoy Prospekt and would take him at least a half an hour to get there. He hoped it was worth all this running around.

"What the hell happened to you?" Bulloch asked the two Englishmen. He had been met outside the apartment building by Kestrel and escorted up to their hideaway. "One day you were there, and the next you were gone! I didn't want to ask any questions in case I messed things up for you. Some of the others asked after you, Peter, but I said that you were probably off on assignment somewhere."

"Some more lemonade, Lucius?" Richard asked, bringing a pitcher in from the kitchen. He poured some into each glass and sat down. John turned from the open window where he had been watching the street below and joined them.

Bulloch looked at them. Peter Pringle didn't look at all like he had when staying at the Astoria. He now had a full beard and moustache and his hair was a different color. Redding had cropped and dyed his hair and had somehow lost his freckles which had been a distinctive mark on his face. He had a white scar on the right side of his face which drew the attention of an observer's eye.

"We failed in our mission, Lucius." Richard told him. "By the way, my name is Richard Cromwell and this is John Kestrel. You might as well know, everyone else does." He added with a touch of sour humor. "We were invited to leave the Country or get shot, we chose this compromise."

"So you're still trying to do whatever it was?"

"We're not sure," Kestrel told him. "It depends, but in looking things over, we found out something else which is why we got in touch with you."

"Can you tell us how your investigation on the missing weapons is going?" Richard asked.

"It isn't." he told them shortly. "We found out how it was done, but that's about all. I have to go official, but I won't get any co-operation. I'm waiting for orders."

"So how did they do it?" John asked.

Bulloch set his empty glass down and looked from one to the other.

"We couldn't think how they could steal arms off of a closed, sealed train. We even had US marines on board! And we had to trust what they told us. My colleague in Moscow did a lot of bribing and a small burglary to gain access to transit papers and he figured it out. They didn't steal the arms, they stole the car!"

He was surprised to see smiles on both his listeners faces. "Somehow, they substituted another freight car and let the whole train continue to here, but here's the funny part. The car didn't stay in Moscow, it came here as part of the original train and was dropped off somewhere in this area.

No one noticed an extra car, at least none of our men did. That was how we found out. The papers showed an extra car leaving Moscow and the right number arriving. God knows where the arms are now, anywhere in northern Russia. I think we'll have to write it off, the only thing remaining is what to tell the Russian government."

"I saw at least part of your shipment this morning." John told him quietly. "They were stacked in a freight car on a siding in the Finland station."

"What!" Bulloch sat bolt upright. "Well let's go get them, or tell someone or something!"

"Why?" asked Richard. "We know where they are, they're not going anywhere for the moment and we have them under observation."

"You do? How?"

Cromwell affected a nonchalant air and stretched out a hand in the general direction of the city.

"Even as we speak, my loyal minions have all under control. Not a sparrow shall fall, but I hear of it."

"What the hell are you talking about?"

Richard grinned at him. "I have formed my own Baker Street Irregulars!"

Bulloch had never read Sir Arthur Conan Doyle and was not acquainted with Sherlock Holmes.

"While John was toiling in the railroad, I went to Spasskaya, you are familiar with it?"

Bulloch nodded. The old haymarket was a warren of taverns and brothels. A haven for deserters and home to the blackmarket in Petrograd.

"In that area are hundreds of children in desperate need. Some beg, some sleep in the streets, all of them steal. For most they have no choice. Their mothers are working, their fathers are in the army or dead. Anyway, I recruited a dozen or so for my own ends. I give them watching jobs, nothing dangerous, and pay them well by their standards. No one pays any attention to a couple of children playing or loafing around, they're part of the scenery. The car with the arms is now under observation from dawn until midnight. As are some notables in this city. Kerensky, Cherkassy, Protopopov and others. Did you know that Leon Trotsky was released from Peter and Paul this morning? I have my lads watching him as well."

Bulloch was impressed and said so. Cromwell shook his head.

"We're just amateurs Lucius, fumbling in the dark. Our mission collapsed and we're trying to save what we can from the ashes. Which brings me to the reason we got in touch with you. John, why don't you tell him what you found this morning in detail?"

Kestrel filled him in on seeing Cherkassy, going to the car and his subsequent fight with the unknown guard.

"What did you do with the body?" Bulloch asked.

"He's now on his way to Kiev." John told him. "Another load of cars came in on the next siding. I waited, then picked the lock on one opposite mine. It was tractor parts bound for Kiev. I made sure that he had no identity on him and when he's found, they won't know where he's from."

"And Mr Cherkassy and his group will be nonplussed as to his disappearance." Richard finished. "Which brings us back to that lovely arsenal sitting in a siding. We thought that we might use it for a small piece of blackmail, if that's all right with you."

"Who do you want to blackmail?"

"Alexander Kerensky." Richard told him with a smile. "Your objective is to find out where the stolen weapons are, and implicitly, to give them to the recognised Russian government. Well, we found them and we'll give them back if he will do something for us."

"What teeny thing would that be?"

"Nothing really. Just transport the royal family to Murmansk where they will be put aboard a British ship bound for England."

Bulloch sat back and looked at the two young Englishmen. They were young, compared to him. He was all of thirty-one and considered himself ancient.

"God, how quixotic!" he said. "This was your mission? The whole of Europe is falling in ruins and you want to save one of the men who caused it?"

John was surprised. "He did? How? I thought the Kaiser had a hand in it."

Bulloch lived in Washington in a responsible government position. He was closer to the seat of power than most. He also had the normal American viewpoint about a people dominated by an autocracy. There were currently in America, thousands of former Russians and Poles who told tales of the atrocities carried out in the name of the Tsar. His Country was now a temporary ally of Russia, but that didn't mean he had to like it.

"The Tsar started the ball rolling by defending the Bosnians and threatening Austria. After that, everyone else climbed on the wagon." He ran his fingers through his hair. "I don't suppose it matters any more who did what to whom. We are all knee deep in blood and it's getting higher." He sighed. "I suppose that one family more or less won't make much difference, how do you want to do it?"

"Well, we're rather counting on you for that." John said. "In the last couple of weeks, Cherkassy has been constantly at Kerensky's right hand. We can't send him a letter, someone else will read it first. We will be recognised if we go there and you can't just breeze into the Prime Minister's office. We were hoping that you could arrange a personal interview with him and let him know the situation."

"But that would involve me in the blackmail." Bulloch protested. "I can turn a blind eye, but I can't be actively involved."

"All right." Richard broke in. "You get an interview based on some urgent information that has been given you. We can give you a letter containing our demand. You just have to make sure that Cherkassy isn't present at the time."

"Do you think that he'll go along with this?" Bulloch asked skeptically.

"Why not? It's what he wants to do anyway. But politically, he's been hamstrung. This way he can blame someone else, get the guns back and patch up a quarrel with America who has been blaming him for the theft."

Richard gave Bulloch an innocent smile. "You're really doing him a favor, and you will sit in very nicely with your President."

"If you put it like that, how can I resist?" Bulloch told him sardonically. "With friends like you, who needs enemies? The letter will have to be carefully worded, in fact the whole plan needs work, it's kind of sloppy, it has a lot of loose ends."

"I quite agree." Kestrel said. "It needs work, but it's just a basic plan. Why don't we go to work on it? I'll go and get some more lemonade."

He paused coming back from the kitchen with the lemonade to see the other two sitting at the table with a pad of paper, their heads close together. He shook himself in disbelief. Here they were. An American treasury agent, an English army captain and a London bobby planning to blackmail the Prime minister of Russia to get the Tsar of all the Russias out of the Country. If they pulled this off, what was next? Kidnap the Kaiser?

CHAPTER TWENTY

"WILL YOU HAVE SOME MORE TEA, Monsieur Kerensky?"

Tsar Nicholas asked. He lifted the pot and Kerensky nodded. They were in the front sitting room of the Catherine Palace overlooking the pond. The girls loved to walk around it, anything to get away from the stultifying effects of house arrest.

"I want to thank you for your lack of action of two weeks ago." Nicholas said in a quiet voice.

They were speaking French in order that the soldier stationed in the room would not understand. Strictly speaking, only Russian was to be spoken to the family, but Kerensky thought he could bend the rules when it suited him.

"I hope that you understand my position." The Tsar continued. "I am an officer in the army and an officer's first duty is to escape, if he can. But I am grateful that no reprisals were taken against my family."

Kerensky grinned to himself. The reason no reprisals had been taken beyond a week of house arrest, was that the whole thing had never happened. Cherkassy's men from Peter and Paul had replaced the regular guards. Only colonel Kobylinsky, Cherkassy and himself knew about it and it was going to stay that way. In one way he had to admire Nicholas for trying. It might have succeeded if Cherkassy hadn't known on which side his bread was buttered.

"I have decided to move you and the family from Petrograd." He told Nicholas abruptly.

The Tsar lit another cigarette and hooded his eyes to keep Kerensky from seeing the sudden hope that flared in them.

"Would it be possible to go to Levadia?" he asked. "As you know, a number of my relatives are already there."

The popular resort on the Black Sea had indeed quite a few Romanovs living there, each with a suitcase packed and a boat standing by.

"I don't know." Kerensky temporized. "I'm going to Moscow tomorrow, I'll make a decision when I return in a week."

He pondered telling Nicholas the truth and decided against it. He didn't think that he could get the family safely to the Black Sea. They would have to pass through some of the most rabid anti-Tsarist towns on the way. The train could easily be stopped and the family forcibly removed for trial and execution. His hold on the army was precarious and almost non existent with the labor Soviets. Kerensky was going to send another train along filled with troops, but he'd just as soon not put them to any test of loyalty. It would have to be somewhere East. As far east as he could manage while still staying in Europe. He got to his feet and bowed slightly to the former monarch.

"I will see you when I return."

"Can you tell me when this will occur?"

"In about two weeks, the middle of August. You can tell the household to be ready, they're all going."

Kerensky was moving towards the door when Nicholas called him back.

"One last question, Monsieur. The two men who tried to help us, what became of them?"

Kerensky shook his head from side to side and smiled at the Tsar.

"No, we didn't shoot them. England is an ally, we don't need any more problems that we have. We sent them home."

He left the room and Nicholas moved to the window watching until he saw Alexander Kerensky come down the steps and climb into his waiting car. The Tsar was glad the two men had lived. The girls would be especially happy. Sunny had prayed nightly for their souls. His thoughts skipped about. It was always betrayal. In both his time and his father's, there had been numerous plots against the throne and they had always been betrayed by someone inside. The Russian anarchist saying was true.

'*When three men sit down to plot revolution, one is a fool and the other two are police spies.*'

He left to go upstairs and inform the family of their imminent departure. Levadia would be good for Alexis, he was always better in the warm sunshine and the cool breezes of the Crimea. It would be a safe place for them and at the same time, it would be easier to take ship from if the opportunity arose.

CHAPTER TWENTY ONE

"YOU'RE SURE?" Lenin demanded. Feliks Derzhinsky nodded his head up and down. "Near enough." He replied.

They were walking in the woods just outside Helsinki. Lenin shivered a little and looked up at the trees shading the sun. The woods that stretched in an almost unbroken line from here up past the arctic circle.

A vast forest broken only by thousands of lakes left by the retreating glaciers. They reminded him of the concert he had been dragged to last night. A performance of Sibelius' violin concerto. He didn't have much of a musical ear, but he'd liked it. To him, the music seemed to spend all it's time in the woods of Finland with only an occasional flash of sunlight coming through the trees.

"Do we know why?" Lenin asked.

"Ambition, power, money." Derzhinsky answered. "It's the key to most men. Yuri Cherkassy wants to get ahead and get rich. Zinoviev knows him. He thinks that he's playing all sides. He doen't dislike you or your plans, he's just looking out for himself. The day the letters were printed in the newspaper, Cherkassy had an interview with Kerensky and the day after he is suddenly restored to favor and now sits at his right hand."

"You must be more ruthless." Lenin told Derzhinsky. "Anyone who is not for us, is against us."

They turned around in the track and made their way back to the farmhouse he had been staying in.

"Do you think that it's safe for me to go back?"

"I think so." Feliks told him. "Kerensky has too many other things on his plate right now. There's no active search for you. The German advance has petered out, mostly because of a massive attack by the allies in Belgium. He's got a small revolt on his hands in Moscow and is off tomorrow to put that fire out. Trotsky was let out of jail yesterday, that's a good sign."

Lenin said nothing. He kept walking along the track with his hands clasped behind him, thinking. They had been so close! He could lose everything they had built up because of that bastard, Cherkassy. It was time to go back and reorganize. It had to be this year! Much of his support came from those that wanted to get out of the war. If Kerensky signed a separate peace agreement with Germany, he was finished.

He snorted with amusement. He was in a peculiar situation. In order to take power he was reliant on the allies persuading his enemy to continue with a war that he, Lenin, wanted to stop!

He believed what Leon had told him when he returned from New York. America was an industrial giant that had now woken up. With their enormous latent power, the war would soon be over. He had read yesterday in the paper that their soldiers had now been in their first battle, a draw.

The Party also needed rifles and the ammunition to go with them. The chance of a bloodless coup had vanished with publication of those letters. Arms were hard to get. Soldiers returning were relieved of their arms at the station and they were reissued to those going up. Everything else was kept under lock and key and heavily guarded. Perhaps a raid on an arsenal? He turned to his companion.

"I want him, my friend."

"You want who?" Derzhinsky was confused.

"Cherkassy of course! I want him snatched out of his house, or off the street, wherever you can get to him. I want some military information from him, then I'm going to kill him, personally." He added for emphasis.

Derzninsky looked doubtful. "That won't be easy. He is well guarded and he's moved into the fortress, surrounded by his own men. If we snatch him, there will be an enormous hue and cry to find him. I can probably have him assassinated, do you really have to speak with him?"

Lenin considered. The information would be useful, but he could probably get it from other sources. What he really wanted was Cherkassy before him begging for mercy and know- ing that he wasn't going to get it.

"Check into it and see what you can come up with. If it's feasible, fine. If not, kill him."

They entered the farmhouse together and he went into the bedroom to pack his few possessions. It would be good to get back.

CHAPTER TWENTY TWO

YURI CHERKASSY LOOKED AT THE BARE DESK with satisfaction. With Alexander away in Moscow he could get things done. As Special Assistant to the Prime Minister, (Temporary), he had almost unlimited power. If he couldn't take care of something in two days, he either pushed it off on someone else or locked it away in a drawer and promptly forgot about it. It had worked just fine in the army and it worked here.

He lit a cigarette and pondered his next step. It was almost time to move on. He thought that he and Kerensky had worked well together. Alexander was at heart a politician, trying to keep everyone happy and succeeding with no one.

Yuri had in a few short weeks made decisions that cut to the heart of the matter that pleased a few and made enemies of others. All in Alexander's name of course. Yuri's mother had borne no fools. In March, when the Revolution had started, he had, by coincidence, been reading a biography of Talleyrand and had taken its lesson to heart.

Talleyrand had been minister to the ill fated French king, then advisor to the revolutionary tribunal, then he worked for Napoleon and still later, for the next short lived monarchy. He had sailed through all these opposing forces while those around him had lost their heads. Yuri was going to make damn sure that he didn't lose his.

He crossed over to the wall and looked at a huge map of Russia. Before he left, Alexander had told him of his decision to move the Romanovs somewhere.

"Give me a short list that I can look over when I return, Yuri. Somewhere quiet and obscure, near the railway and far away from any extremist elements."

His finger traced the rail line from Moscow east to the Urals and the beginning of Asia. His eye went further to the other side of the divide and followed the track of the trans Siberian railroad. Most of Russian industry and hence it's revolutionaries, were west of the Urals. His eye traced the course of the long river Ob down from the arctic circle and paused where another river split from it, the Irtysh. There it was, the perfect place! Tobolsk. Far away from everything and involved with nothing except it's own survival. First thing in the morning he would find out more about it.

Cherkassy rang down and ordered his car to be brought around. This job carried some perks with it. He now had a car and a driver at his disposal. He sat in the back and watched the passing scenery on the short drive to the Peter and Paul. He had thought it prudent to move in after his mini coup. If the Bolsheviks ever found out what he had done his life would be a short one. Unless, unless,—maybe it was time to even the scales again.

The car swept through the fortress gates and it's time of arrival was noted by two men industriously laying brick cobblestones in the same hole that they had dug them out of. Feliks Derzhinsky's men were looking for an avenue of approach. Cherkassy's arrival and the two men were also noted by three boys playing with a tennis ball and three old brooms. Cromwell's Irregulars were also on the job.

CHAPTER TWENTY THREE

At 10am on the first Tuesday in August, Lucius Bulloch entered the building that housed the US Mission to St Petersburg. He introduced himself as an American and asked to speak to the person in charge. After the inevitable shuttling back and forth he eventually found himself seated in front of Mr Clarence Depp, Special Assistant to Mr Elihu Root who had since returned to America.

Mr Depp was a somewhat florid man with thinning brown hair and sporting what had become known as a 'Kitchener' moustache. A gold watch chain strained across his ample stomach as he leaned forward to inspect the card that Bulloch handed to him. He looked at the card then at Bulloch, his eyebrows raised.

"What brings you here so far away from home, sir? Aren't you supposed to be protecting the President?"

"That is indeed one of our duties, sir, but we do have others including forgery and arms control.

That is the reason why I and some others are here in Russia."

It hadn't worked out the way that Cromwell and Bulloch had planned. Yesterday he had gone to the Tauride Palace hoping for an interview with Kerensky only to find that he was in Moscow and would not be back for a few days. They were shot down before they started.

Back in the Astoria, he considered his options. Initially, he had had no objections to going along with Cromwell, they were allies and his objective would be fulfilled by a roundabout road. Kerensky being away messed it up. By his estimate, only half of the arms stolen were in that box car in the siding and they could be moved at any time. Mindful of his position as an American government employee, he thought his best bet was to explain the situation to someone higher up and seek direction. He told Clarence Depp some of the truth, but not all of it.

"So you see the position, sir. Our people are in a line stretching from San Francisco to Vladivostock to here. By chance, I seem to have uncovered the location of the arms, or soon will. I am due to meet with the informant shortly and he will demand payment for the location after I receive some proof. This is the only office here with sufficient funds to supply me and I have no time to wait until Washington approves."

This last had been a sticking point with him, but Richard had been adamant.

"Neither Kerensky or anyone else will believe your story unless some reward or ransom is being demanded. With the state of affairs here, it's practically mandatory. We can figure out what to do with the money later, although I'm somewhat short of funds, Cherkassy got most of it."

Clarence Depp leaned back in his chair when Bulloch had finished and laced his fingers together over his paunch. He looked away from Bulloch at the wall as though seeking inspiration. His eyes came back to Bulloch.

"Very interesting, sir! I'm very glad that you brought this to me. It only underscores Mr Root's belief on the state of affairs here. I'm surprised that we didn't know of it."

"Probably because you were on your way here when it happened and Mr Wilson didn't think that it would affect your negotiations. Just guessing, sir."

Clarence Depp's eyes inspected the ceiling this time and it seemed to help. He snapped forward in his chair.

"All right, Mr Bulloch, here is what you do. I'll arrange for you to receive the reward money, but be damn sure that you are getting the real McCoy. When you know the location, bring it back to me and we'll take it from there."

"Shouldn't I inform the Russian government?"

Depp leaned back in his chair and his face grew sharp and his eyes cold.

"Under no circmstances will you tell anyone but me anything! Is that clear?"

Bulloch wasn't an idiot, it was very clear; but he wanted to make his point.

"My orders from the President were also clear, sir. If I, or any of the others were to find anything on Russian soil, we were to inform the Russians and let them take it from there."

Depp changed his tune and leaned forward giving Bulloch an avuncular smile.

"The situation has changed since the President gave you that order. Things that he could not have anticipated have taken place. You've been here for what, six weeks? You know what it's like here.

Mr Root is most concerned. He feels that the Russian army has no more will to fight and that everything will soon disintegrate. There might even be a civil war! And in such a struggle, it is not our policy to arm one side or the other. At the moment, I think that our best choice might be to blow the whole lot up! So, tell no one and we will decide what to do. A great deal will depend on the location of course and who has present charge of them."

Bulloch knew who had charge of them, but he sure as hell wasn't going to tell this smooth operator a damn thing. He might also have handed information to the President's internal foes in Washington.

It might be in their interest that the arms remain missing.

"I understand, sir. I will report to you once I have the information." *Like hell I will!*

"I'm glad we understand each other, Mr Bulloch." Depp was all smiles now. "If you will return here later this afternoon, I will have that authorization for you."

No handshake from Mr Depp, only a regal wave of the hand. Bulloch left the building filled with chagrin. He had needlessly complicated things out of a sense of duty and patriotism. He consoled himself with the thought that he would soon be receiving rather a lot of money. Perhaps it was time to look out for himself.

CHAPTER TWENTY FOUR

FELIKS DERZHINSKY LOOKED OUT of the side window of the car at the glistening cobblestones in front of Peter and Paul. The rain, drumming on the roof, seemed a good omen. This would be the third time they had tried this. In the last week he had gone over Cherkassy's movements carefully and this was the only point where he was vulnerable.

Since Kerensky's return from Moscow, Cherkassy had been busy implementing the flurry of orders that had piled up. He went to work in the morning and returned in the evening with no outside excursions.

The square in front of the fortress was a stage to Derzhinsky. All the pieces were in place, it only remained for the lead actor to come on stage. The first time had been a dry run, but yesterday had been for real. At the last possible second he had aborted, traffic conditions hadn't been right. This time it looked good, the rain would make it easier.

The driver grunted and he looked through the rain to see Cherkassy's car approaching. Only seconds to make up his mind. "Do it'" Feliks told the driver.

The driver flashed his headlights twice and the first car pulled out just in front of Cherkassy's vehicle, causing it to slow down a little. As both cars entered the square, a second car followed by Derzhinsky's vehicle pulled out and approached on a collision course. His number one and two cars came together with a satisfying bang and everything stopped.

Cherkassy's car stopped behind the first car and his car stopped behind the second one. The square was now blocked in both directions. The few pedestrians around took one glance and scurried for shelter out of the rain. The drivers of both cars got out and started waving arms at each other, shouting.

Derzhinsky could see Cherkassy leaning forward looking out of the front window, his chauffeur shrugging and speaking over his shoulder. One quick glance at the guards outside the fortress, they hadn't moved.

The two drivers began exchanging blows as the passengers in both cars got out and drifted casually back towards Cherkassy's car, one standing beside the chauffeur's seat and the other at the rear door. Derzhinsky got out into the rain, opened the rear door of his own car and nodded.

The rear door of Cherkassy's car was opened and Cherkassy was pulled out, given a quick clip on the head with a sand-filled sock and hustled dazed, over to the open door of Derzhinsky's car and thrown inside. Derzhinsky climbed in beside the driver who immediately reversed, made a sliding U-turn on the wet street and drove off.

Looking out of the rear window, Derzhinsky could see the drivers and passengers of the crash cars jumping into their vehicles and beginning to leave the scene. Leaving only the chauffeur and the fortress guards who were only now beginning to move. He sat back with a satisfied grunt, the whole thing had taken less than a minute.

The car drove over the bridge on Bolshaya Ulitsa, then over Bolshaya Nevka, a tributary of the Neva, and into Vyborg. The district of Petrograd filled with factories, tenements and most of the poor working class of the city. The home ground of every revolutionary party in Petrograd for the last twenty years.

Yuri Cherkassy, awake but still dazed, was held pinned in the back of the car. A blindfold was put around his eyes and all he could do was listen to the rumble of the tires on the stones of the street. The car made a sharp left turn and stopped. He was pulled out of the car and guided into a building and up some stairs.

From the hollow echoing sound of their steps Yuri guessed that the place was empty. He was pushed down into a chair and he felt ropes going around his arms and legs. Behind the blindfold, his mind was working rapidly. There was only one bunch who would have kidnapped him, Lenin and the Bolsheviks.

Somehow they must have found out about his ploy with the fake letters. He was a little surprised to find himself still alive. Lenin was not known as a forgiving man. They must have some reason for keeping him in good condition. He didn't know how long he had before they questioned him, he'd better think of something fast.

Yuri sat in darkness and silence for about an hour before the sound of the door opening and footsteps brought him to the alert. Hands released the ropes and the blindfold was taken off. He blinked at the sudden influx of light from the overhead bulb and looked up. Three men were standing in front of him. Two he did not know, but the third was Feliks Derzhinsky.

Feliks studied him for a moment then went back to the wall, brought forward a chair and sat down facing him. The other two retreated out of the light to the doorway. Derzhinsky brought out a packet of cigarettes, offered him one and carefully struck a match to light it, putting the box back in his pocket. Yuri took a grateful draw on the cigarette and smiled at his enemy.

"Hello, Feliks. I hope you have a very safe place here. By now, the army and the police should be combing the city looking for me. At a guess, somewhere in Vyborg? An abandoned apartment or factory? There can't be that many."

Derzhinsky gave him a bearded smile and shook his head at him.

"Why did you do it, Yuri? I thought of you not as a friend perhaps, but at least neutral. I thought you realized the historic inevitability of our cause."

Yuri laughed at him. "Historic what? That's shit, Feliks and you know it. Keep that stuff for the students." He shrugged. "It was just business."

They were interrupted by the door opening and Lenin came into the room and walked forward into the light.

"What was just business?" he asked.

Yuri took a last draw on the cigarette and let it drop to the floor. He had thought about it in the darkness of the blindfold. For once, he couldn't come up with a plausible excuse or blame anyone else.

"You of all people should understand, Vladimir Ulyanov. I didn't write those letters, but they came into my hands. You will use anyone and anything to gain power for yourself and the party. I just did the same thing for myself. I gained great favor by my actions. I dealt you a temporary setback, but at the same time placed myself in a position to help you."

Lenin snorted in amusement

"To be sure! It was all for my long term advantage. We will send you back with apologies and you will faithfully send me such snippets of information that you think will be useful."

Derzhinsky drew out a British Webley from his jacket and offered it to Lenin.

"Do you want to do it yourself?"

Lenin took the gun and turned it over in his hand, fitting his finger in behind the trigger guard and looked down at Cherkassy. Yuri looked up at him and the green eyes smiled.

"Go ahead and be dammed to you!"

Lenin tossed the gun back to Derzhinsky.

"No, I've lost my appetite for it. You do it. Put the body back in the car and toss it out in front of the fortress. It will give Kerensky something to think about."

He turned into the darkness then, with his hand on the door handle, turned back.

"No, wait a moment." Two strides back. "There is something that could save your life, Cherkassy. Something that you could tell me."

Yuri let out his breath slowly. He had been waiting for this, the reason he was still alive. He didn't believe Lenin for an instant. He would be killed the moment his usefulness was over, but that would be later and while there was life, there was hope.

"What is it that you want?"

"I need the plans and means of entry into one of the city arsenals."

Cherkassy laughed at him as he had laughed at death.

"You're clutching at straws! If you are asking me, you must have studied it and know that it's impossible. Why do you think that returning soldiers are relieved of their weapons immediately?"

Lenin said nothing, just looked at him.

"Well, there are two reasons. First, they are needed to reissue to soldiers leaving and second, the government wants to make damn sure that no group like yours can get their hands on them. Why do you think that one crack regiment is always kept in the city? Well you already know why.

Without false modesty, why do you think that I was in charge of Peter and Paul?" He looked up directly at Lenin.

"I must have hurt you more than I realized. You've been counting on a popular revolt to overthrow the government and now you don't think that you can make it, you want to do it the old fashioned way, with guns."

Lenin was hearing back what he knew to be true. What Leon and Feliks didn't want to tell him. Without some terrible blunder by the government, he was finished, his dream smashed. His eyes became cold.

"If you can't help me, I have no incentive to keep you alive." He turned to Feliks. "Put a rug or a blanket in the car, we don't want to spoil the upholstery."

"I didn't say that I couldn't help you, only that you're going about it the wrong way." Yuri turned his eyes to Derzhinsky. "Find another chair for the comrade and give me another cigarette, I've got a story to tell you."

This time he lit the cigarette for himself and looked about for somewhere to put the match. The guard at the door brought an ashtray for him. He flicked the match nonchalantly into the container. He was running a bluff and had to carry it off with true Russian insolence. He had to establish control.

"I know where there is a container half filled with new revolvers, rifles, mortars and the ammo to go with them." He told them. "There's also some TNT."

"Where?" Both men asked simultaneously.

He sat back in the straight chair, feeling the bars against his back and flicked some ash away.

"Well, there's a problem. I tell you that it's in such a place. You go there and make sure that it's true then Feliks here puts a bullet in my head. That would not make me happy. I need some guarantee. I give the location to you and it wipes out any animosity between us. I wanted them for myself, but in the present situation, I give them to you." He shrugged delicately. "What do you have to lose? Like you, I wanted to be one of the pieces, not a pawn. It's not worth it for you to renege on an agreement,

I might be very useful in the future. It's just business."

It galled Lenin to admit it, but Cherkassy was right. He had to put the Party ahead of his own wishes. Besides, if he let him go, he wasn't going anywhere, he could always find him again. What was one man's life against taking over the Country?

"Where do these arms come from"

"They were part of an American shipment. I stole it. Half of it is in Moscow with some of my brother officers, the rest is here in Petrograd."

"All right, we have an agreement. Where are they?"

Yuri stood up and found to his surprise that his legs were a little shaky. He fixed Lenin with a cool glance.

"Not quite that fast, comrade. Now that we're all friends again, I wouldn't want to put it to the test. I will need two cars. Feliks, myself and your guards will all drive together to the spot. He will give me the key to the extra car and I will wait with one guard while he checks my story. He signals the guard and I drive off. Simple, no?"

To Yuri it was simple. He got out of this room and immediate execution. He would be in the open with only one guard to overcome if anything went wrong. He was sorry to lose the shipment, but he could always steal some more, or steal it back.

"Now," he said with confidence. "We have to concoct a suitable story about my daring escape from the nameless ruffians who abducted me. Then we'll be on our way to make you master of all Russia."

If there was one thing that Lenin had learned in all his years in exile, it was patience. He had been patient in Siberia and in London and in Switzerland. He was filled with a sense of purpose and a conviction that he had been put here to make it happen. Nothing would stand in his way, certainly not the life of an opportunistic Russian officer. His time would come.

CHAPTER TWENTY FIVE

IT WAS PAYDAY in Spasskaya. Richard Cromwell had set up in the back of a small cobbler's shop in Apraksin Dvor, a maze of tiny shops, stalls and kiosks just off Sadovaya Ulitsa. The cobbler was well paid to take a break for an hour.

The children came in one's and two's to tell their stories. He listened to each one gravely, taking notes and sometimes asking questions. He thought that this had been a brilliant idea. Children see far more than adults realize, it just has to be interpreted. He was forming a very complete picture of what was going on. He wasn't privy to any secrets, but the results were mirrored in the effects on the townspeople. The kids all adored him. He treated them like adults and paid them into the bargain.

He was almost ready to go when Miki and Toni burst into the tiny shop agog with news. The man they were to watch for at Peter and Paul had been kidnapped! They had seen it all. Two cars had crashed into each other, the man dragged from his car and driven off in another one. Destination unknown but it went in the direction of the bridge into Vyborg. He paid them and told them to wait outside while he packed up and left the money for the cobbler. He was thinking furiously.

Cherkassy had been snatched. The conclusion leapt out at him, it had to be the Bolsheviks. If they hadn't killed him outright, they must want something. There was only one thing that Yuri could use to buy his life.

He bought both the kids a lemonade at a kiosk while considered the best course. John wouldn't start work for over an hour yet, he would still be at the flat. He wrote out a note, putting it in English for safety.

Cherkassy taken. Join me at the hill overlooking the yards where the wagon is. There should be a cab downstairs. Drop the kids off on your way.

He walked up Sadovaya to the Nevsky Prospekt with the kids in tow and started looking for a cab. In Petrograd at this time, most of them were still horse drawn. He found one, bundled the kids inside and gave the driver his instructions.

"Take them to this address and wait for them. They will come out with a man. Bring the boys back here then go wherever the man tells you."

Richard gave the driver enough money, watched them trot off then turned and walked down the rest of the Prospekt to where it ended at the station.

Richard hated to give away the location of the flat to anyone, even his Irregulars, but this was an emergency. He worked his way through the maze of side streets behind the station until he could enter the park and climb the hill that overlooked the marshalling yards. There wasn't much cover, but it would be easier when it got dark. He walked along the ridge until he came to the siding that had the wagon with the armaments. It was the third car from the end. He wondered if Cherkassy had replaced the guard.

Richard looked behind him, the ground there was flat and trampled. It was probably used by local kids to play football. Beyond the field was another road leading up to the field. It was gravel and wide enough for a car. If Yuri did what he thought, that was the way they would come.

At this end of the field, near the edge of the escarpment, was a boxlike structure. He walked over to examine it. It was a small park shelter with a slanted roof supported by two thin partitions and a back wall with a long bench open to the field. Nailed above it was a long board with faded lettering on it. He could just make out "—artak FC." There was no cover inside. Anyone sitting there would be seen in an instant. Richard walked back to the edge and looked down to the yards. There were engines backing and filling in the mysterious pattern that only yardmasters know. The downslope of the hill offered no cover, just shale and scree falling down to the rail lines.

A squint into the setting sun gave him an estimate of half-an-hour to dark. He went back to the small shelter, sat down and lit a cigarette and waited.

Just as the last rays of the sun were disappearing he heard noises coming up from the direction of the yards. He stood up, walked over to the edge and looked down. It was John and Lucius Bulloch scrambling their way up shale to join him. The two arrived at the top and he stood back to give them room. John caught his breath and said,

"Lucius happened to be at the apartment when your messengers arrived and insisted on coming along. Why are we here?"

Richard led them back to the shelter and they sat together on the bench facing the field and the long ago triumphs and tragedies of Spartak Football Club.

"Because this is where they'll come. The Bolsheviks must have him and this is the only thing he has to sell, this location. They won't kill him until after they find out if he's telling the truth."

"Are we talking about the same man?" Lucius asked. "The one who threatened to shoot you if he saw you again?"

Richard nodded to him with a smile, then shrugged.

"Right now in this place, we are in a time of shifting loyalties and Yuri can shift his with the best of them. Do you really want the Bolsheviks to get that arms supply down there? I didn't know what else to do, so I came here and hoped that John might come up with something."

He gestured with his hand. "As you can see, there's nowhere to hide. I hoped that perhaps we could move the freight car before they got here. Is that possible?"

John shook his head. "Not in the time available. It's impossible to move cars without the yardmaster knowing it." He opened the satchel he had brought. "I did bring something else though."

John reached in and laid three guns on the bench before them. They were Smith and Wesson revolvers. He reached in again and brought out a box of ammunition to put beside them.

"Where in heaven did you get these?" Richard cried, then realized. "Oh."

"Exactly." John smiled. "There was one crate practically full of them and I thought they might come in handy. I only took one box of ammo, if we need more than that, we're dead anyway."

Bulloch picked up one of the guns, broke it open and began to load it from the box.

"Well, we can certainly give someone a hell of a surprise." He said. "But where can we hide until then?"

Lenin had augmented Yuri's plan. He had added a truck to the caravan.

"Why waste time?" He had told Derzhinsky. "If the stuff's there, take it while the going is good, or as much as you can."

Yuri, sitting in the back of the lead car, was getting worried again. There were now four men plus himself, two more than he had counted on. He had omitted to tell Lenin that there were now two men on permanent guard in the car since the disappearance of Andrei. The situation was promising although in the event of a fight breaking out, he might get shot before he could get away.

The headlights of the car bounced their way up the gravel slope to the old football field and shone past the deserted hut and into the blackness over the hill. The lights from the shunting yard shone up and the toot of whistles could be heard. The three vehicles moved out abreast on the field until they came to the edge of the downslope, where they stopped.

"Kill the lights." Derzhinsky ordered. "We don't want to be noticed up here."

Three engines stopped and the lights were put out. The three drivers, Derzhinsky and Yuri all got out of their vehicles and walked over to the ridge. Yuri was looking about him in the dark, seeking a suitable escape route, but he could see nothing.

"Which is it?" Derzhinsky asked.

"It's the train nearest us, the third car down from the left."

Derzhinsky nodded to two of the drivers.

"Take flashlights and go down and check it out." He held out his hand to Yuri. "The key."

"In return for the car key." Yuri told him.

They traded keys and the two drivers started down the slope to the train. Yuri began to walk towards the second car, but was stopped by Derzhinsky's voice. "Hold it!"

Yuri turned into the flashlight shining on his face.

"You stay right where you are until I say go. Klem, keep your gun on him. If he does anything at all, shoot him."

On the rail line, hiding behind the second car, John heard the sound of the two men half sliding down the slope and drew his gun. He assumed that the two men he had heard talking in the car had also heard.

Behind the faded -artak FC sign on top of the shelter, Richard and Lucius Bulloch were lying on the roof, listening as the two left. Richard was playing this by ear. If they tried to take away any of the arms, he would stop them. If they tried to kill Yuri, he would stop them.

In this dim, half-lit war, he didn't have many friends, and Yuri was not among them, but he was more of a friend than an enemy. The moon came from behind a cloud and lit up the area. Bulloch turned his head to Richard and lifted his hand, palm up, questioning. Richard shrugged.

Everything changed in an instant. Down by the railcars, two shots rang out, followed by another. Derzhinsky stiffened and drew a gun from his pocket. He glanced at Cherkassy, who looked surprised.

"Shoot him!" he told Klementi.

Cherkassy, with nowhere to go, spread his arms wide.

"Wait a second! We don't know what is happening!"

Klementi said nothing, but lifted his arm with the pistol and aimed directly at Yuri's heart. In the moonlight, Yuri could see the gun barrel lining up and poised himself to jump, even though it was too late. The sound of the shot shattered the darkness and Klementi's face disappeared in a spray of moon-black blood. Yuri's jump turned into a roll which fetched him up alongside the fender of one of the cars. Yuri came upright to see Klementi's body sag tiredly to the ground.

Derzhinsky, expecting the shot, was a little late in realizing that it was not Klementi who had delivered it. He started to turn and look upwards just as Richard launched himself from the top of the shelter and landed directly on top of him. The force threw him to the ground where he was half stunned.

Richard completed the job by tapping him smartly on the head with the butt of the gun.

It seemed longer but the whole thing had only taken two seconds. Now time started to return to normal. Bulloch put the gun back in his pocket and climbed awkwardly down from the roof.

Richard, on all fours beside an unconscious Derzhinsky, got to his feet breathing heavily in the cool night air. Cherkassy looked with incredulity at his two rescuers, two dim figures in the moonlight, and took a step towards them. Without thinking, Richard called to him.

"Yuri, get out of here!"

Cherkassy checked and started to turn away. He stopped again and looked back at the caller. Tall, blond hair shining in the moonlight, a full beard. That voice!

"English? Is that you, English? Is that you, Captain Cromwell?"

CHAPTER TWENTY SIX

RICHARD IGNORED CHERKASSY for the moment, cursing his slip of the tongue. He turned to the edge of the hill and stared down into the partial darkness. What about John? Who had fired the shots that had started all this? Bulloch came to join him and they heard the scrunching noise of feet coming up the hill.

Three shadowy figures began to appear, one of them supported by the other two. Light streamed out before them and Richard realized that Cherkassy had put on the headlights of one of the cars. As they came to the top of the hill, Richard saw that one of men was John with the arm of a stranger around his neck. He kept his gun out but held it down by his side. Kestrel stopped at the top.

"Give me a hand, will you? He's heavy."

In the headlights, Richard could see the stranger's shirt was covered by blood in the chest area. Bulloch came forward and between them they eased the man to the ground where he groaned as his head hit the earth.

Richard looked at the stranger bleeding on the gtound and at the other standing beside John.

"Who the devil are you?" He asked.

"They're both mine." Cherkassy's voice came from behind. "They were the guards that I left here. What happened to Derzhinsky's men?"

"Both dead." Kestrel told him. "I was watching. They opened the car door and shone a light inside. They must have seen the men inside. One of them shot into the car and these two shot back. They're both dead beside the track. Now what do we do?"

"It's a mess." Richard told him. "I've got Feliks Derzhinsky lying out cold over there and another body. You have two bodies beside the train and two live guards and we all have Yuri Cherkassy standing behind me who now knows that we are still in Russia. I'm not sure where Lucius fits in, but we'll think of something."

Cherkassy came from the darkness to stand beside them. He looked at Richard.

"I have never been so glad that someone disobeyed my orders. I owe you my life captain." He looked at Bulloch. "Who's this? Ah! I've seen you before somewhere, an American reporter no? No matter. I have a lot of questions, but I think we'd better do something about this battle site, don't you?"

"As I said before, Yuri, I think you had better get the hell out of here." Richard told him. "You also have a wounded man to take care of. Let's get everyone into the truck. I'm sure that you can find a place to get rid of the bodies." He looked at Derzhinsky who was groaning and beginning to sit up. "What are we going to do about him?"

Cherkassy shrugged, unnoticed in the darkness.

"He was going to kill me a few minutes ago. I'm not too sensitive about his feelings."

"Do you have any rope in the truck?" John asked.

Cherkassy went back to the truck and rummaged about, returning with several lengths of rope.

"Tie him up and put him in the football shed." Richard ordered. "Blindfold him as well. I don't want him to see any of us."

Cherkassy left with one of the cars and his wounded man, promising to return as soon as he had him attended to. The four of them went down to the train and retreived the two bodies putting them in the back of the truck. Cherkassy's man left with the truck promising that the bodies would never be found.

The three of them gathered at the edge of the hill and looked down at the shunting yards and the train with it's lethal cargo sitting there.

"We have to do something about that." John said. "Cherkassy will want to move it, Lenin won't give up and both of them know that someone else knows about it."

"Why don't we blow it up?" Bulloch suggested. Mindful of the advice offered by the Embassy man. "It's the middle of the night, well away from traffic. This way, no one gets it."

"All right," Richard agreed, "but let's take a few items first. They might come in handy."

Half-an-hour later, they had almost worn a path going up and down the hill. Cromwell and Bulloch had put together one crate of assorted weaponry and lugged it up to the trunk of the remaining car. There were no fuses included in the shipment so they had had to improvise. Straw from the crates was sprinkled about and a cloth trail was laid leading from the car up the hill. The whole lot was liberally doused with petrol from the spare tank kept in the back of the car. John looked behind him to the shed where the hapless Derzhinsky was sitting.

"You know, this is going to create a hell of a bang. Will he be all right you think?"

Richard looked down to the siding and back up to the shed and shrugged.

"Who cares? When that lot goes up, it's going to attract a crowd, he's certain to be found. Alive or dead he'll be a lesson to the Bolsheviks and the beauty of it is that Yuri will get the blame for it! Why don't you two get in the car and get it started. I'll light the trail and join you. We want to be a good way from here when it goes up."

Richard stood in the darkness marvelling at the silence. With all that had been going on, no one had investigated. Shots fired, lights all over, up and down that bloody hill. He supposed the neighbors were used to the train sounds going on all night.

He heard the sound of the car starting and lit a match from the box, kneeling down to see that the cloth caught fire. It started with a yellow flame and raced down from the hill faster than he had imagined. He ran to the car and jumped in. "Let's go!"

At the bottom of the hill where the houses started, they met Cherkassy coming back and waved at him to follow them. They drove quickly through the maze of side streets to the front of the station. Both cars pulled up, Cherkassy jumped out and went to them.

"What's the big hurry? Did something happen?"

Well behind the station a monstrous sheet of fire rose in the sky followed by a tremendous blast. Fifty people outside the station froze in their tracks and looked upward.

Time seemed to hang in the air like the bits of rolling stock silhouetted against the sudden light before the world crashed in again and gravity took effect, dropping pieces of debris in a half mile area. Cherkassy stood stock still oblivious of the ash and debris raining down on him.

"You blew it all up!" He accused Cromwell. "There was a small fortune in there."

Richard nodded at him, his face aglow from the secondary fires now lighting up the night sky.

"It seemed the best thing to do." He laughed at Cherkassy's face. "Cheer up Yuri, at least the Bolsheviks don't get it and you can always make another fortune."

Screams and shouts now penetrated as people recovered from their temporary paralysis. The sound of breaking glass as part of the dome over the station collapsed.

"I hope no one was injured in there." John pointed to the station exit which now had people streaming from it.

"I think we'd all better get out of here." Cherkassy told them. "The police and the army will be here at any moment." He looked hard at Cromwell. "I have a few dozen questions for you, but they will wait until morning. We need to talk. Don't worry, I'm not going to shoot you or have you locked up, I owe you too much and it looks like my plans have blown up in my face." He smiled ruefully.

"All right." Richard told him. "The café outside the Mariinsky theatre this afternoon at four. Don't bring any company."

In the distance they could now hear the strident clamor of bells as the fire department and two ambulances came barreling down the Nevsky Prospekt. Richard looked at the people outside the station. There weren't any bodies and there wasn't any blood that he could see. Most of the damage would have occurred in the yards, they would have to wait for the papers in the afternoon.

"What are you going to do?" he asked Yuri.

"I'm going to my office and announce my daring escape from the German saboteurs who kidnapped me and blew up something in the station. It should get me some sympathy and win a few more points with Alexander for being on the job. And you?"

John yawned and everyone else did the same.

"I think we're all going to bed and get some sleep. It's been a busy day." Richard told him.

The three of them climbed back in the car and roared off leaving Cherkassy to consider again how his fortune and his life seemed to be bound up with this Englishman who looked so much like him. Two army trucks squealed to a stop and he thought he'd better make himself scarce. They would round up everyone and he needed some time to think about his next move.

CHAPTER TWENTY SEVEN

LUCIUS BULLOCH SAT BACK in his chair and tried to look modest as praise from Mr Depp rang in his ears.

"I'll give you this much, sir." Depp continued. "You got value for the money we paid you. I have only one small question. I thought you were going to come here first and tell me when you knew where the arms were?"

"The situation didn't permit it, sir." Bulloch told Mr Root's deputy. "You told me to be sure that my informant really knew where they were. The only way he could do that was to show me, which he did. At the same time, I learned that the cargo was to be shipped that night. There was no time to let you know. Rather than start over again, I took your advice and blew the lot up."

Clarence Depp knew when he had been out-manouvered. It was time to retreat.

"When I report to Mr Root, I will be sure to let him know of your action in this matter and that in my opinion, you did the best thing in the circumstances."

"Thank you sir," Lucius murmured. "I was sure I could count on your support."

He left the American enclave with a spring in his step and the knowledge that his share of the bribe money would keep him fairly well off for a year.

Alexander Kerensky and Yuri Cherkassy sat opposite each other in Kerensky's office. The morning's newspaper spread on the table beteween them.

"Thank God no one was killed." Kerensky said. "Twenty-three wounded, mostly by flying glass and none seriously. You're sure it was German saboteurs?"

"Fairly sure." Yuri told him. "At least the people who kidapped me spoke German and I assume the two events were connected."

"Why you?" Kerensky wondered. "What could you give them or tell them?"

"Fortunately I never got the chance to find out. They left me alone long enough for me to wriggle out of the ropes and escape. I wasn't about to hang about and find out."

"Find out for me why we had explosives there in the first place. I'll have someone's head for it. How much damage was caused?"

"Not much. Two train loads completely destroyed. One badly damaged. Some track blown up, but that can be repaired quickly. The shunters at work in the yard were lucky. The locomotive engines protected them from the blast. One engine was partly blown off it's tracks. We should be back to normal operations by tonight."

"All right, on to other things. I've decided to take your recommendation about a destination for the Romanov family. Tobolsk looks just fine to me. I'd also like it done as soon as possible, say this weekend? The 14th or the 15th?"

"That only gives me a few days." Cherkassy protested. "It will take some time."

"Why? Get two trains, pick out some good guards and off they go."

"It won't be that easy. Trains don't run by themselves, you need engineers and the railway workers Soviet may not be too happy about taking the former Tsar and his family anywhere. Also the guards may not be overjoyed to take an extended holiday east of the Urals, plus I'll need some money for food and supplies."

Alexander Kerensky thought about it. It was more difficult than he had expected and secrecy was important. He wanted the family gone before anyone in the city knew about it.

"All right. Pick out fifty good men along with Kobylinsky. Issue them new uniforms and weapons. Make sure that they have been paid up to date and promise them a bonus for this duty.

Tell them that I'll have another detachment sent out and that they'll be home by Christmas. You might hint that this will mean that they will be unable to fight on the front against the Germans. How many railway workers will we need?"

"A minimum of six, three to each train. An engineer, a fireman and a conductor unless you want the train to keep going without a stop, then we'd have to increase that to allow for sleeptime and breaks. You have to have two relief firemen anyway, call it eight."

"See to it personally, Yuri Stepanovich. I want no one in the Duma or elsewhere to hear about this in advance."

"I'll take care of it right away." Cherkassy promised.

He knew damn well that it would be almost impossible to keep it a secret once the railwaymen heard about it. Only promises of heavy bonuses might delay it. He looked at the clock on the wall as he left the office. It was almost three-thirty. Time for his appointment with the English captain.

Cherkassy had been waiting for ten minutes at the café outside the Mariinskiy Theatre before the waiter brought him a note from Cromwell redirecting him to a small bistro in Spasskaya. It seemed that the English captain was not about to trust him too much. Yuri couldn't blame him.

He had been at the bistro for only five minutes when Cromwell and Kestrel slid into the booth beside him. He put down the newspaper he had been reading beside his empty tea glass.

"Satisfied?" he asked.

Cromwell nodded. "So far. You came alone. What do you want Yuri?"

"Nothing much, except to thank you again and to satisfy my curiosity. Why didn't you leave Russia when I gave you the chance?"

John ordered some tea for them both and gave Cherkassy a flat stare.

"We English are almost as stubborn as Russians, Colonel. We take exception to being run out of town. We thought we'd stay around for a few weeks and take in some of the local sights."

Cherkassy knew what that meant; intelligence. Nothing specific, just keeping one's eyes and ears open. Catch the mood of the people, the results of laws passed. Was there rationing? Was Russia reaching the bottom of the barrel in manpower? Britain was an ally, but you never tell allies everything.

"Just as well for you that we did, Yuri." Richard told him. "The other man that you met last night? The American? He's not a reporter, he's an agent of their government. He was sent to look for the arms that went missing and he had you down as chief suspect. He recruited us to keep an eye on you. Turned out to be right, didn't he?"

Cherkassy was satisfied. He had had suspicions that the two had stayed to make another attempt to rescue the Family. Now he had the evidence of his own rescue to back up their story.

"What are you going to do now?"

"Nothing, we're leaving in few days." John told him. "The American's job is over, he found what he was looking for and took care of it in his own way, with our help."

Yuri sat back and lit another cigarette from his case.

"I'm glad to hear it, gentlmen. I had the notion that you might still be after the Family, but that doesn't matter any more."

"Why not?" Richard asked. "Just out of curiosity."

"Because with your help, I finally succeeded in persuading Kerensky to get them out of town; they're leaving very soon."

Richard gave John a quick sideways flick of his eyes. John lifted one eyebrow in response. He hadn't heard about it in the yards, of course he hadn't been there for a day. He would be there this evening.

"That's interesting, Yuri. Where are you sending them?"

Cherkassy opened his mouth, then closed it with a snap. He smiled at them both.

"Oh no, English. I've told you too much already. I merely wanted to put your minds at rest.

You can tell whoever sent you that they will be safely out of the way until the present power struggle is settled."

"Why are you being so nice to us?"

Cherkassy smiled again and waggled his right hand up and down.

"You know how it goes. You never know when you will need a friend. If I had shot you the last time, you wouldn't have been able to rescue me. Perhaps we can help each other in the future."

"Aren't you afraid of repercussions from last night?"

"Not too much. Lenin is a realist. When he fails at one thing, he goes back and waits until it is time to try something else. I didn't betray him to Kerensky, there is no warrant out for his arrest and he will know that I could have done so if I had wished."

"So we're all done?" John asked getting ready to leave.

"Just one thing more." Cherkassy told them looking at each of them in turn. "I have very good contacts in a place where a certain Family will be held. When you get back, have Bruce-Lockart in Moscow get in touch with me. It could be to your advantage."

"Who?

Yuri laughed at them both. "Come on, gentlemen! We are not complete idiots here. When Kerensky took power, the first thing he did was examine all the files on our allies and all foreigners in Russia. We know that he is more than a Consul here. I'm not complaining, everybody does it. I prefer to keep my lines of communication and my options, open."

Cherkassy bade them both a courteous goodbye and walked out into the late afternoon sunshine thinking somewhat smugly, that he had done a good day's work.

Back in the café, John laughed and shook his head.

"He's a cool customer, isn't he? He's got every angle covered."

"There's one he doesn't, John. He fell for our story about Bulloch because it was logical and he had the proof. You have to try and find out when the family is leaving and their destination. The Grenville will be back in Murmansk in five days and this time, we really have to be on it. This is our last chance to do anything. With some luck, we may give Yuri the surprise of his life!"

CHAPTER TWENTY EIGHT

JOHN KESTREL CAME HOME just as Richard was having breakfast. They had fallen into a routine. John would have something to eat and fill Richard in on the latest word before going to sleep.

Richard would then become Yevgeni, Captain of the Irregulars, and send his troops out into battle. He was feeling less like Sherlock Holmes now, more like Fagin sending his urchins to steal information from the pockets of the city. He would linger for a while in the stalls of Spasskaya, listening to the casual conversations of shoppers, the gripes of wounded soldiers and especially to deserters who had gone to ground in the warren. They knew what was really happening at the front.

The black market was a font of information. What was in demand indicated what was in short supply. Then over to the Palace Square in front of the Winter Palace. The foot of the Alexander column had become the Hyde Park Corner of Petrograd. Speakers drunk on their own rhetoric declaimed on every subject to a mostly bored, unemployed audience.

After generations of repression, the idea of being able to say just about anything in public hadn't worn off yet. Then he would swing over to the Tauride Palace, to the seat of government and see who was coming and going.

The impressions of the city, the people and the government were soaking in, but he knew that it would be difficult to explain to anyone in Intelligence. They wanted facts, pieces of paper. How many armies? How armed? What ordnance?

Everything he had learned pointed to the same thing; Russia didn't want to fight any more. There was a bone tiredness in the people that transcended patriotism. If the Germans were actually at the gates, that would be a different matter, but they were far away in a part of the Country that wasn't really Russia and the people who lived there didn't think so either. They wanted an end and anyone who could give them that would have their approval.

"The trip that Cherkassy spoke of," John mumbled, his mouth full of bread, "the word came through last night. They're looking for volunteers for a long trip. Four engineers and four firemen. Extra pay. They won't say where, but the guessing is east of the Urals. Two trains to leave on Saturday. I'm going to take a short nap then go back this afternoon and speak to some of the men on the day shift and see what more I can learn although I don't see what good it does."

"Nor do I." Richard confessed. "I just think that we should look it over before we go. The Grenville will sail from Murmansk on Monday, we can at least go back with up to date information."

That afternoon, he met Lucius Bulloch outside the Winter Palace and they sat down for tea.

"I'm leaving Russia on Monday." Bulloch told him. "I've got a cabin on the Grenville, a British ship sailing out of Murmansk. My masters are happy with me and I am summoned home. I've never been to London and I thought I'd go via the Atlantic"

"John and I will take you sightseeing." Richard told him. "We're on the same ship. I assume that I will be given some leave before rejoining my regiment. By the way, don't expect much in the way of service on the ship. It's not a liner, it's a navy cruiser on escort duty to merchant ships."

"I don't give a damn as long as it helps to get me home. I'm sorry your trip was waste for you and John."

"I don't think it was. We will probably spend a week being questioned about conditions here. It's been very interesting being back."

"Back? You've been here before?"

I spent a good part of my childhood here. In St Petersburg, not Petrograd."

He smiled in reminiscence and told Bulloch a number of stories of childhood adventures in the city.

"Of course, looking back it seems nicer than it actually was. I had no cares or responsibilities. I was not aware of the turmoil going on and the persecution."

"I never thought that my Country would be an ally of Russia." Bulloch said. "It is the antithesis of everything we stand for. I suppose war makes strange bedfellows."

He stood to go. "I look forward to seeing you on the train to Murmansk and I'll take you up on that sightseeing offer."

Richard was up early the next morning and prepared breakfast for John and himself. He was anxious to know what more he had learned of the departure of the Tsar and his family.

"They are having a few problems." John told him after breakfast. "No one wants to go!"

"The word leaked out of course. It's an open secret that the Tsar and his family will be on the train. The yardmaster even offered more money, but he got no takers so far. Some of them genuinely hate the Tsar and others are afraid of guilt by association. If the train gets stopped by an angry mob en route, they could get killed. I've seen a couple of mobs in London. No one listens to you and just doing your job is no excuse."

Richard could now appreciate Kerensky's problem. The Country was already starting to split into fiefdoms. Some western towns were being run by the Soviets and were a law unto themselves. They obeyed orders from Petrograd and Moscow if they felt like it.

"Tell me about the arrangements."

"There will be two trains leaving on Saturday. One will go to Tsarskoe Selo and pick up the family and servants, about fifty people. It will then steam back up the line to the little circle where the other train filled with about fifty troops will be waiting.

The second train will then fall in behind the first and the two will be off in the direction of Moscow. No one knows where after that. They could continue east to the Urals or south to the Black Sea."

"What's the little circle?"

"There's no rail line through the city." John explained. "If you come in from the north to the Finland station and wish to continue your journey, you have to take a taxi over to the other station and get the train from there.

However, to move rolling stock and freight, they made two circles around the city, the little circle and the big circle. They bypass the city and join up with the Moscow line on the other side."

"And the line from Tsarskoe Selo is not on the direct Moscow Line?" Richard asked, interested.

"No, it's a branch line. On the way down, its direct. On the way back, where the little circle joins, there's a switch point and an arc joining the main line. In former times, if the Tsar was staying at Tsarskoe Selo and wished to go to Moscow or anywhere along the line, he didn't have to come into the city, just have the points switched at the circle and keep going."

Richard thought about that, the germ of an idea growing. He fetched a pad of paper and put it in front of John.

"Can you sketch that? It will give me a better idea of the layout."

John took a pencil out of his pocket and closed his eyes for a second, visualizing the map of the rail system. He started one sheet, looked at it, tore it up and began another. Richard made them some more tea and waited patiently until he was finished. John pushed it across to him.

"This is roughly what it looks like. I've left out a lot, if you need more detail, I'd have to look at the map in the yardmaster's office."

Richard looked at the sketch, his elbow on the table and his right hand around his chin. The green eyes pensive and his mind working in overtime.

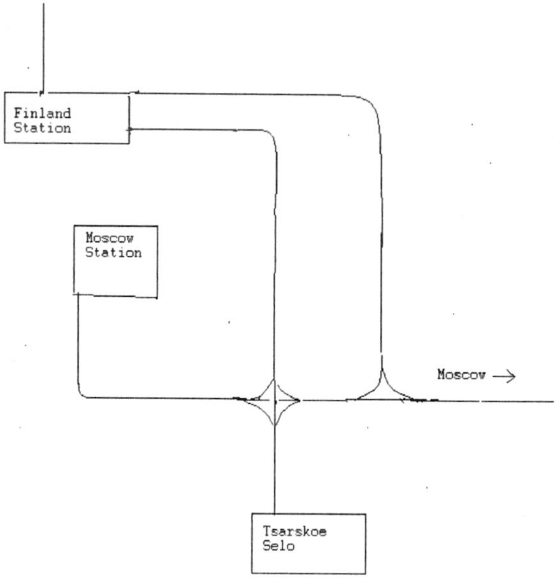

Richard's nail traced the line up from Tsarskoe Selo to the junction and right to the Moscow line.

"What's the timing on the second train? The one with the guards."

"It will wait in the station until the yardmaster receives a call that the first train has left Tsarskoe Selo. About fifteen minutes later, the train will leave and steam to this point."

John's finger touched the map just short of the junction with the little circle. "They will be able to see the first train approach and take the Moscow line, then they will cross over the points and fall in behind."

"Will there be any guards on the first train?"

"I don't know, I shouldn't think so, only Colonel Kobylinsky. What are you thinking about?

Holding up the train and getting the family off? It's impossible."

Richard whistled softly between his teeth as he looked at the rough map.He looked up and grinned at John.

"Actually, I'm wondering if we can steal the train!"

CHAPTER TWENTY NINE

"STEAL THE TRAIN?" John echoed. "Brilliant! What are you going to use? Vanishing cream? It runs on rails you know."

"Well, not really steal it, just disappear it for a little." Richard pointed with his finger. "What's the distance between the points going to the little circle and the points of the big circle?"

"About quarter of a mile. Enough to let a long train get on to one set of tracks before getting to the next switch point."

"I was thinking that if we could delay the arrival of the second train, we could run the first one on to the big circle, then when the second train arrived, they would think that the first one was just ahead on the Moscow line."

"Richard, that involves three impossible things." John sighed. "But let's ignore them for the moment. All right, you have the train on the big circle, what then? It goes only to one place, Finland Station. Once the train enters the Finland complex the yardmaster will have a fit seeing an unauthorized train steaming in. It can't be rerouted through to the Murmansk line, only his people up in the box can do that. He'll be on the phone screaming bloody murder to someone in the Moscow station who will realize what has happened."

"All right, let's think again. There must be some villages alongside the track there. Could we have a couple of cars waiting at one of them? The train stops, the family gets off and then steam the train right into the Finland Station unattended. That should create some chaos."

John was reluctantly caught up in the idea, but shook his head.

"It's a marvellous idea, Richard, but I have to bring up my three impossibles. First, we have to find a *very* obliging engineer and fireman who will stop the train, switch the points then stop and switch them again."

Then we have to find two cars and have someone drive them to the transfer point. Last, how do we delay the departure of the second train?"

Cromwell waved his hand airly and smile at Kestrel.

"The first is no problem, John. That's you and me! You told me they are looking for volunteers. So you volunteer if your brother in law can be the fireman."

"You owe him money that you can't pay, and this will take care of your debt. You don't need skill to shovel coal. If they are that hard up to find people, it should be no problem."

Next, we steal two cars and place them in the right place. For that, we need the help of our American friend, Lucius Bulloch. I'm sure if we ask him nicely he'll go along. That's two out of the way. Now we just have to find a way to delay the second train. What about stopping the call from 'Selo?"

"Won't work, Richard, you've been there. The stationmaster's office is surrounded by glass, anyone can see in and on that day it's going to be busy, very busy. Someone, probably Colonel Kobylinsky, will give the order to the stationmaster to phone ahead that the train is leaving. Any delay has to be at the other end."

"We've got that explosive that we stole. We could put a dent in the tracks after they get the phone call, that would slow them down."

"No good." John shook his head. "They would guess immediately what was happening and send a messenger down the track or phone to halt the train. It has to be some delay that while it's exasperating, is understandable. How much time do you think we need?"

Richard looked down at the map on the table, counting.

"We stop the train, change the points, run the train on to the big circle, stop again and go back to change the points back then get out of sight. I'd say a minimum of half an hour, but the more the better."

John also looked down at the map, seeking inspiration then his head came up and he smiled.

"You know, there's real doubt among the workers about letting the Tsar leave. Here, they feel that they have a measure of control. That's one reason they have difficulty in finding people. It occurs to me that there hasn't been a decent demonstration of the Railway Workers Soviet in months. Don't you think that it's about time?"

Richard grinned back. "Very nice! An angry group of workers blocking the tracks and refusing to let the train leave. I like it!" He frowned. "But how do we arrange it? and even more, how do we time it? Since we won't be there."

"Arranging I think I can do." John told him. "I'm fairly well liked at the yards since I am able to find silk stockings and foreign cigarettes on the black market and at a great price! There are two people I could talk to who are important in the Soviet. I'll go and see them this afternoon with a bottle of something."

"It's the timing, though." Richard worried. "We need it after the phone call comes through and not before." A thought struck him. "This is going to be done in daylight, isn't it?"

"Who knows?" John shrugged. "This is Russia, there's no such thing as the 9.15 from Paddington. Trains move at the whim of whoever controls the departure. However, one of the men I am going to talk to works in the yardmaster's office. He would know when the call comes in. If you go and find Lucius, I'll take a nap before setting out again."

He sat down on the bed to remove his boots. Were they realy going to try and steal a train? One last desperate gamble before going home. Home? He'd almost forgotten about London in the last six weeks. No, not forgotten, just put it somewhere in the background like a place you visited once. The door closed as Richard left and he covered himself up with a sheet leaving his clothes on.

"I can't do it by myself." Bulloch told Richard. "Two cars need two drivers and where the hell am I going to find two cars? They're in short supply here and they all belong to someone. No, wait a moment. There's a fat little bastard called Depp at the American legation who has one. I've seen him drive it. He's the one who gave me the money."

"I happen to know where there's a beautiful 220K Mercedes in a lockup." Cromwell told him cheerfully. "The owner will be busy on Saturday, I can almost guarantee it."

"I do have a problem." Bulloch told him, almost embarrassed. "I don't know how to steal a car without the keys. I wouldn't know how to start it."

"I can take care of that." Richard told him confidently. "There are plenty of thieves in Spasskaya who will do most anything for money. I'll find one who can bypass the starter and bring him to you."

"Then what?" Lucius asked.

You go with this man to Depp's place and steal his car, then you go to the lockup and get the other one, after that you both go the village that I'm going to pick out and leave them there. If all goes well we'll see you the next day in Murmansk to board the ship."

Bulloch was shaking his head in doubt.

"Jesus, Richard, I don't know. Yes, Hands Across The Sea and all that, but I have no desire to see the inside of a Russian jail."

"How would you like to be known as the American who saved the Russian royal family? The American papers will make you a hero. The President will have to promote you and the Russian royals, who are all over the place, will forever be in your debt."

The prospect stiffened Bulloch's resolve and he nodded.

"All right, but I won't leave you. I'll wait with the cars and we'll all go together."

Richard frowned. "This isn't the Three Musketeers, Julius. If a wheel comes off, we'll all be shot.

You can be well out of it, waiting for us in Murmansk."

Bulloch shook his head stubbornly. "No, you might need me, these people have no idea what to expect, how do you look after four young girls, an invalid boy and shoot out of the rear window at the same time?" He grinned at Cromwell. "All for one and one for all! Besides, do you know how to bypass the ignition on a car? I will once your villain has taught me."

Cromwell's sea-green eyes glinted with affection for the Treasury man And he reached out to clasp his hand. "All right, you're in. I'm going out there this afternoon to pick a spot, do you want to come with me?"

"I still think you made a mistake volunteering, Ivan." Georgi Kristol slurred the words as he passed the bottle back to Kestrel. John pretended to take a swig of the liquid and put the bottle back on the ground at the side of the bench.

They were sitting together at the top of the hill overlooking the yards. The same place where the encounter with Cherkassy and Lenin's men had taken place. It was getting dark and and a fog was creeping in. Mournful toots could be heard from the yards below. John thought that Georgi would never see that he wasn't drinking, if he even cared.

"Someone had to do it, Georgi. I don't have a woman to keep me warm at night and I can use the extra money. Besides, If no one volunteers, they will just bring in people from the army to run the train. There must be plenty of conscripts who have worked on trains and would jump at the chance to get away from the front."

Georgi looked about for the bottle in the gathering gloom. John passed it to him. He would have to go down soon and get to work.

"You're not drinking!" Georgi accused.

"I have to go to work, you've just finished your shift."

Georgi considered that. "That's fair. Leave the bottle when you go. I don't know how you get this stuff, it's fantastic!"

"I was thinking Georgi, how about a demonstration on Saturday when the train leaves? Shake up the bosses."

"Damn good idea, Ivan! We still have the banners from last time. Give the Romanovs a last goodbye."

"I was thinking of something better. How would you like to see Kerensky himself come and make promises to you? He forgets about the workers now that he's so high up. We should teach him a lesson."

Georgi took another swig from the bottle and held it up to the waning light to see how much was left.

"How would we do that?"

"Simple. You work with old Vladi in the office. When the phone call comes for the second train to leave, you pass the word for the demonstration to start. Everyone stands in front of the train and refuses to leave until Kerensky himself comes to the station to talk to you."

Georgi belched and nodded his head up and down.

"S'good idea. Wait a bit, suppose they run the train over us?

"You're drunk, my friend. Genadi's the other driver, isn't he? Do you think he's going to run over his friends and fellow workers?"

"All right. You come and see me tomorrow when I'm sober and we'll set it up. We'll give the bastards something to think about!"

"I'm only sorry that I won't be there to see it, Georgi Timofeovich. But I'm sure that you'll do a magnificent job. You can tell me all about it when I get back."

John left Georgi up on the hill with the remains of one of his last bottles and walked down the track to the yards thinking that he had sown the seed well. A follow up tomorrow would clinch it. For the first time, he had the feeling that this scheme to steal the train and rescue the Tsar and his family might actually work.

CHAPTER THIRTY

RICHARD CROMWELL LEANED ON THE DOOR of the engine cab and looked backwards down the platform at Tsarskoe Selo. Where the hell were the royal family and their entourage?

John and he had brought the engine down here at eleven this morning. They had coupled up the cars of the royal train and then watched as numerous people had gone back and forth supplying the train with all it would need for its long journey across Russia to Tobolsk. Since then, nothing.

Two hours sitting here in regal splendor. The engine gently hissing to itself as John did mysterious things to keep the pressure up. Richard had taken a short tour through the train out of curiosity and had been overwhelmed by the splendor and opulence of the cars.

The royal compartments were as luxurious as the palace itself along with a complete kitchen with an attached cold car. The Tsar's father had not believed in roughing it. Even the servants quarters were plusher than the hotel room they had had in Petrograd.

The phone rang in the glass windowed office of the stationmaster and he saw that elderly gentleman pick it up and listen. He saw his head go up and down a few times then he replaced the receiver, looked up and saw both John and Richard watching him. He opened the top half of the dutch door and leaned out.

"They're finally coming! Get ready!"

John nodded back and turned to wipe an imaginary speck of dirt from the controls.

"What's to get ready? We've been ready for two hours." He muttered to Richard. They were both a little nervous, so many things could go wrong.

Lucius might not be able to get the cars, the demonstration might not come off, there might be an armed guard put on the train, although so far there had been no sign of any. Richard disliked plans that relied on things outside his control, but had had little choice.

From outside the station came a low rumble and quickly the station was changed from it's somnolent summertime state to a crowded, almost frenzied condition. Cars and trucks appeared in the square before the station entrance. A hundred or more people had suddenly arrived and were joined by the curious from the village itself.

Trunks were brought off trucks and put on the train in one of two luggage vans. People bustled back and forth with mysterious objects loading an already loaded train. Valets, footmen, cooks, maids, bottle washers and general dogsbodies bustled about in organized confusion.

The local guards, who weren't going anywhere, barked orders which were ignored. Richard suddenly saw the family coming on to the platform accompanied by three ladies-in-waiting, a sailor pushing young Alexis in a wheelchair and Colonel Kobylinsky. He turned away and tended to the coal. He didn't want Kobylinsky to see him and make any connections. The bustle went on for another half-an-hour until with a note of finality, the last door was slammed shut. John, polishing the dials in the cab, kept an eye on the stationmaster's window and saw him pick up the phone and speak into it. That had to be the phone call to Petrograd.

He nudged Richard who followed his gaze to the glass covered office and saw the stationmaster put on his blue coat with red trim and step outside. Richard put down his shovel and leaned on the cab side watching him. The man strode down the side of the cars to the end of the train and turned until he was facing forward to the front. He lifted a small whistle to his lips and blew a strident blast, a green flag waving from his right hand.

Standing in the waiting room, Yuri Cherkassy watched the green flag wave up and down. He was still in a vile temper. Yesterday, Alexander had told him to go down the Tsarskoe Selo and make sure that everything went off well. He had decided to drive down himself and this morning had gone to the lockup for the Mercedes and found it gone!

There had been no time to investigate, he had had to find a car and a driver to bring him here. But when he got back to Petrograd, he was going to move heaven and earth to find who had stolen it and mete out suitable punishment. He was torn between impalement and boiling in oil.

Today he was in full uniform and wearing all his medals. The Prince might have banished him, but he couldn't take away the recognition that Yuri had received from his comrades. He lit a cigarette and watched the train begin it's first slow jerking movements as the couplings took up the slack. He gaze wandered idly down the train to the cab and he saw the fireman swinging his shovel filled with coal and disappearing as he bent to push it into the fire. It was only a glimpse, a fleeting glance and the head went out of sight, but it was enough. Without quite knowing why, Yuri flung away his cigarette and ran out of the waiting room just in time to board the last car.

"What the hell is the matter now?" Kerensky snarled into the phone. "I thought we had everything settled."

"It's something new sir." Said an anxious station-master. "We have a demonstration by the railway workers. They've crowded in front of the train and they won't let it leave until you come and talk to them."

"Hold on."

Kerensky held the phone in one hand and his eyes went upward in search of divine intervention. This was turning into a circus. He had wanted a quiet, no fuss departure and there had been one obstacle after another.

First no one had wanted to be in the guard detachment and now this. He had no doubt that it was a political ploy by the union to show him that he had better get along with the Soviets or else. The question was, should he bend to it, or ignore it. In the end, expediency won out. He had to get the family off his back and out of harm's way.

"All right," he told the stationmaster. "I'll be right there."

There was quite crowd at the station platform when he got there. Most were bystanders seizing the opportunity to stop working and see what was going on, but there was a crowd of about fifty on the tracks in front of the train. Two banners with *"All power to the Soviets"* waving over them.

Most of the fifty-five guards were either on the platform or hanging out of the train windows watching with amusement. He briefly considered ordering the guards to clear the tracks and dismissed it, they might not obey him. The stationmaster bustled up to him.

"Thank God you're here! Will you talk to them? They're getting nasty."

"Has the signal come through from Tsarskoe Selo yet?"

"Yes, about fifteen minutes ago. The train should have left by now. Will you talk to them?" He repeated.

Alexander Kerensky strode to the head of the train and stood beside the engine, looking down at the men on the tracks. There was a roar as he was recognized.

"Bring out the German woman!" Came some cries. Along with, "Keep the Romanov's here!" and "The hell with the Tsar!"

He looked to his left. There was a narrow walkway running down the side of the engine from the cab to the front. He grasped the steel bar and hauled himself up to the cab and from there on to the walkway. He sidled down the edge until he reached the front of the engine and was standing about six feet above the workers standing on the tracks. He raised his arms above him shouting,

"Comrades! What is it that you want? The Romanov's are leaving!"

"Keep them here!" Came one cry. "Why should they live in luxury in the Crimea?"

"They're not going there." He retorted. "I am sending them to a place of greater security." He dropped his voice, forcing the crowd to be quieter.

"I recently uncovered a German plot to free them and further divide our divided nation." He waved a hand behind him. "This train is filled with loyal guards who will ensure that such a thing will not happen again. Do not prevent them from carrying out their important task."

That shut them up. The crowd was muttering to itself.

"Put them in Peter and Paul!" Came another shout.

"I considered it." Kerensky told them. "But there are many spies and paid agents in the city, as we all know."

He couldn't resist getting in that dig at Lenin. "I thought it better if they were far away and out of reach to anyone who is an enemy of the Revolution. Please Comrades, let me continue with the work that you have entrusted to me, let these men continue with theirs and let the Romanov's be far away from here!"

He had them, he knew it. There was some grumbling, but the crowd on the tracks gradually melted away. The banners were rolled up and the bystanders drifted off back to work. Kerensky clambered off the engine to the platform and nodded to the young captain in charge of the guard detachment.

"Get your men back on the train Captain, and get out of here."

The stationmaster was effusive in his thanks.

"I hope that I did the right thing in calling you."

"It's all over now." Kerensky patted him on the arm. "The train will leave, the Romanovs will leave and I am leaving, back to my office to attend to more important matters. It worked out all right."

He strode to the station entrance as the luggage guard blew his whistle for the train to leave. He glanced at his pocket watch. Not too bad, he thought. We only lost about half an hour.

CHAPTER THIRTY ONE

THE TRAIN SENT BACK a long plume of smoke as it steamed through the hot Russian countryside in the direction of St Petersburg. In the cab, Richard laid aside his shovel and wiped his coal begrimed face with a small towel. He glanced at John who was staring ahead through the glass porthole.

"How much longer?" He shouted to make himself heard above the sound of the engine.

"About five minutes." Came the reply. "Keep an eye out on your side for the signal."

Four minutes later, John saw the glint of the cross rails in the sun and the signal mast set at green. They came to the gentle curve that would put them on the Moscow track and he cast an anxious look to the left in the Petrograd direction, no train was in sight. He gave a gentle sigh of relief, one stumbling block crossed. John grinned at him.

"By God, Georgi did it! the train's late!"

The train slowly clickety-clacked its way across the points and straightened out. John slowed the train, keeping a sharp eye out for the beginning of the big circle. He drew the train to a gentle halt and pointed ahead.

"Off you go, Richard, she's dead ahead."

Cromwell clambered down to the track and walked up about twenty yards past the gently steaming engine to the switch point. He grasped the iron swing handle to move the points over and pulled. Nothing happened. He pulled again, putting some force in it, it still wouldn't move.

He looked back at the waiting engine and saw John leaning out of the cab with his arm back in a throwing motion. A metal object flew through the air and landed at his feet, it was an oil can. He squirted some oil into every moving part that he could see and tried again. With a small groan, the points moved over. The way to the big circle was now clear. He waved at John who waved back and the train started slowly forward.

Richard stood back a little from the track and waited as the engine and it's attendant cars moved slowly past him on to the circle. He thought he saw some faces peering out at him from the compartments as they moved past. When the last baggage car had passed the points, John slowed down and stopped. Richard pulled the lever back to it's original position. Now when the troop train caught up to them, they would continue on their way to Moscow thinking that the royal train was somewhere just up ahead, if they had enough time to get out of sight.

He looked back the quarter of a mile to the first junction point, so far no sign of the second train.

The train whistle gave a little toot and he hurried forward. It was time to board the train and tell the Tsar and his family what was happening. He grinned to himself as he climbed on to the step of the baggage car. They were going to get a hell of a surprise!

Yuri Cherkassy closed the door of the baggage car behind him and turned to look about him. Tsarskoe Selo station was slowly receding behind him. He still wasn't sure why he had done this. Now he would have to ride the train until the first station on the line and call back for his driver to come and pick him up.

There were two men in the car looking at him. The train conductor was an elderly man, sixty or so, and a young blond giant that he guessed was the relief fireman. They looked at him with some alarm and he smiled at them.

"No cause for alarm men, just taking a little ride as far as the nearest station."

He took a little time to talk to them, finding out their names and how they came to be on the train. It was a habit he had had since he joined the army. Yuri had personally known every man under his command. It paid off handsomely in loyalty when it counted. He thought he'd better report to

Colonel Kobylinsky. He wasn't a bad fellow, just an unrepentant Tsarist.

Yuri strolled through the baggage car and into the second, marvelling at the number of possessions that the family were taking with them into exile. Then into the narrow corridor that stretched down the length of the train stopping a footman and asking him for Kobylinsky's location. He was told that he was with the family in the lounging parlor, three cars down. He had almost reached the end of the car when he heard the noise of the wheels change as they rattled over the points.

Yuri stopped to look out of the window and saw the train was curving to the right. He frowned as they began to straighten out, where was the other train? He could see the rails stretching back to Petrograd and no train was in sight. Then the train stopped and he relaxed. They must be waiting for the other train to come into sight.

He went into the next car which was the kitchen and walked down it's length stopping only to watch two cooks whipping up something for dinner. The train lurched into motion again and he felt it curving to the left. That wasn't right. He looked again out of the window and saw the engine ahead of him turning on to another track away from the line to Moscow. Something was definitely wrong, he could feel it.

Then he saw the reason for his hidden anxiety. The fireman was on the track leaning against the switch bar ready to turn it as the last car passed. It was the Englishman Cromwell! Everything clicked into place. He *had* recognized him at the station. He had dismissed it but had boarded the train anyway, following his feelings. Yuri passed through to the next car and began to run. He had to get to the family's car immediately. He didn't know what was going on, but he had a shrewd suspicion.

Richard boarded the train at the second baggage car and passed through the next two compartments. The two people he met en route ignored him. He passed the kitchen and the sleeping quarters and pulled open the door to the parlor car.

He had seen it before on his previous walk through, but now he paused to admire it's opulence. It was a miniature palace room with sofas and easy chairs dotted about and two short serving tables and a complete dining table with silverware gleaming on it, set for dinner. This time, the room was crowded. The girls were sitting on two sofas facing each other. Alexis was in a smaller chair with his mother standing over him. The Tsar was standing with Kobylinsky at a bar set almost at the end of the car. Kobylinsky was behind it making drinks. The Tsar was in front leaning on a cane. All the heads turned to look at him as he came into the car. He saw the Tsar's eyes widen and his head turn to a chair. The occupant had his back to him, but he turned as well and rose to his feet with a gun in his hand. It was Yuri Cherkassy!

"Come in, Captain." Cherkassy gestured with the gun. "And please take out your gun slowly and put it on the floor."

"I'm not armed." Richard told him.

It was true enough. He had taken his gun out of his belt when stoking the engine and had left it in the cab. He lifted his shirt and turned around once to show him.

"Very well, you will stop this train at once."

The others were looking at him with dawning recognition. This coal streaked peasant was the dashing English Captain who had tried to rescue them last month. Richard looked at Cherkassy, shrugged and dropped his hands.

"I can't, Yuri. You should know that. Only the baggage guard and the engineer can stop it. There's no emergency chain on Russian trains. Anyway, it doesn't matter, we'll be stopping in a few minutes anyway."

"We will? Why?"

"To take the Tsar and his family off, of course." Richard gestured at the gun. "You may as well put that away, Yuri. There's nothing you can do. I have a dozen men and transportation waiting to take the Family away."

He was exaggerating by eleven men, but Yuri wouldn't know that.

"I could always shoot you and make a stand here. The other train can't be that far behind. Your work I assume?"

Richard smiled and waggled his hand up and down.

"These things happen, delays are endemic in Russia." He looked closely at the gun. "A battlefield souvenir? It's German, automatic, takes a clip of eight. You shoot me, that's seven left. What then?"

Cherkassy scowled and glanced at Kobylinsky who had been as still as the others.

"Are you armed, Colonel?"

"Not here, in my compartment, one gun, six bullets."

The train began to slow down and for once, Yuri wasn't sure what to do.

"They wouldn't dare fire on this car, they might hit the Family." Yuri told Richard defiantly.

"They're not going to fire at all." Richard told him with perfect truth. As far as he knew, Bulloch had nothing to fire with.

"They don't know that there is a problem. When the train stops they expect me to come down from the car and escort the family to the transportation." He wondered if Yuri knew that John was the engineer, any edge was better than none.

The train whistle gave a double toot and the train halted. Cherkassy, keeping one eye on Richard, leaned down to look out of the window. Richard did the same. The view was not prepossessing.

Two low, one story houses with a dilapidated shed some feet away. Lucius Bulloch was standing in front of a black American touring car smoking a cigarette. The 220 K Mercedes was parked in front of the shed. Cherkassy turned to Cromwell.

"You stole my car!" He sounded indignant.

"I only take the best." Richard told him, smiling.

Cherkassy peered out of the window again.

"Where are all these men of yours? I don't see them."

Richard gave an indifferent shrug. "Waiting in one of the houses to see me get off. They won't do anything without pay. It's so hard to get good help these days, it's the war."

Cherkassy made up his mind. He would stall things as long as he could.

"All right, you and I will walk to the car entrance and you will step down from the car, but go no further or I'll kill you. Call the men to come and get their money. I want to see just how many are in your merry band."

Cherkassy had just called his bluff. The last card he had to play was John. If he had realized that something was wrong, he might be waiting outside the car.

"One more thing, Yuri. We must take one member of the family with us. They will want to see that we have been successful."

Cherkassy glanced at the family still in the same positions that they had been in when Cromwell had entered.

"Colonel, will you keep order here while we go outside?" He waggled the gun in the general direction of the Tsar. "Nicholas Romanov, you come with us." The colonel would have no trouble with five women and a boy.

With Cherkassy bringing up the rear, they left the car and stood together at the carriage door at the beginning of the corridor.

"English, you open the door and step down, Romanov, you show yourself at the entrance, wave and step back behind me."

Richard did as he was told, trying to see out of the corner of his eye if John was lurking about. All he could hear was the hissing of the train and the sound of cicadias clicking in the trees overhanging the houses.

Lucius straightened up as he saw him appear and began to wave, then everyone heard it. A long mournful toot from a train whistle coming from behind them and across the fields. The other train with the guards had arrived at the crossing and was either trying to find them or could see them and was asking what the hell they were doing there.

Time was racing down a fine line to an end point. Richard heard it and knew that they only had minutes to achieve their objective. John Kestrel, standing in the shadows between the two cars heard it and wondered why Richard was so hesitant. Yuri Cherkassy heard it and knew that he had won if he could stall things for a little longer. He looked at the cars baking in the late afternoon sunshine and knew what to do.

"Where are all your men, English? I see only the American reporter."

He lifted the gun muzzle from its aim at Cromwell's back and sighted at the touring car where Bulloch was standing. The shot cracked loud in the air and silenced the cicadias. He had been aiming at the rear tire, but missed. The bullet slammed through the rear fender and punctured the gas tank. The second one hit the tire with an explosive bang. Bulloch, startled, threw away the end of his cigarette and ran for the cover of the shed. Cherkassy shifted his aim to his beloved Mercedes and his finger tightened on the trigger.

From behind him, the Tsar's cane smashed down on his wrist, in agony his fingers opened and the gun fell. It was caught before it reached the ground by John who had jumped forward at the sound of the shot. He reached upwards and caught Cherkassy by buttons on his tunic and pulled him down from the car steps to sprawl on the ground in front of Richard.

The gas that had seeped from the punctured gas tank reached the smouldering end of Bulloch's cigarette and ignited, racing back with tremendous speed to the tank itself. The car blew up in a ball of fire sending debris in a fifty yard radius and a black cloud of smoke into the air.

Cherkassy stayed where he was on the ground and the other three joined him until the rain of car parts stopped.

There was a complete silence for thirty seconds until one cicadia started a hesitant chirp and was joined by another. Then they heard three sharp toots from the second train.

"They've seen the smoke and know where we are." John told them, rising to his feet. "As soon as they change the points, they'll be here. At a guess, we have ten minutes."

Cromwell and Cherkassy got to their feet, Cherkassy holding his arm to his chest.

"I think he broke my wrist." He told them. He glanced behind him at the Tsar still standing in the doorway. "What did you do that for?"

The Tsar looked at him with sad, spaniel eyes.

"I thought it was the right thing to do." He told him.

"Jesus Christ!" Came from Bulloch, coming towards them from the cover of the shed. He glared at Cherkassy.

"You damn near hit me!" He skirted the smouldering wreck and joined the others. "What the hell do we do now?"

Richard took stock of the situation. The Mercedes appeared unharmed and it was a big car. He looked up at the Tsar standing in the carriage doorway. Kobylinsky was now standing beside him and he could see Alexandra's face behind them both.

"Sire, we have to get out of here right now! The other train is approaching, we only have minutes."

Richard was calculating as he spoke. There was Bulloch, John and himself, that was three. The car would take three more at a pinch.

"I can take you, your wife and your son. They will never harm the girls."

Nicholas retreated back from the doorway and Richard could see him in a sudden heated discussion with Alexandra and Kobylinsky. He re-appeared in the doorway.

"Captain, we thank you for your efforts on our behalf, but as I told you when we first met, we had already decided that we will not be separated. We all go, or we all stay."

Richard was in an agony of indecision, what to do? There was no time left to argue the matter.

"Then at least give me your son. He will receive the best of care in England."

That seemed to give Nicholas some pause. He stepped back into the car and there was some more discussion with Alexandra. He came back to the top step.

"Both my wife and myself thank you from the bottom of our hearts. It is a hard decision to make, but we cannot bear to be separated from him. We will all be together in Tobolsk and soon Russia will forget all about the Romanovs and we can live simple, uncomplicated lives far away from the struggle that is tearing my Country apart." He smiled unexpectedly. "But it was a grand adventure, was it not?"

Richard smiled back and nodded his head.

"It certainly was. I will give your regards to your cousin."

He gave the royal couple a short bow and turned away to go to the Mercedes. Lucius Bulloch and John were already seated in the car with John in the driver's seat. He had his hand on the door to open it when a voice came from behind him.

"One moment, English." It was Cherkassy.

Yuri had done a lot of thinking in the last few moments. It was true that when the second train arrived he would be a hero, but heroes lived short lives in the new Russia. It was time to change sides again. He had the feeling that life in Paris would be much more interesting and longer, than life in Petrograd.

"As long as you have some room in the car, will you take me with you?"

Richard stared at him in astonishment, then the sound of a train whistle came to his ears.

"That probably means that they have changed the points and are on their way." John said. "We have only minutes."

He laughed at Cherkassy and beckoned, opening the car door.

"What are you hanging about for? We have a boat to catch."

The Tsar, Nicholas the Second, former Emperor of all the Russias, lit another cigarette and looked at the Mercedes disappearing in a cloud of dust. He closed the carriage door and walked back to join the rest of his family.

CHAPTER THIRTY TWO

RICHARD CROMWELL CAREFULLY DEPOSITED his empty tea cup in it's saucer as John was ending up.

"And that's just about the whole story, sir." Kestrel finished.

London, Whitehall, one of the myriad offices of the War Department. The two had arrived the previous evening at Victoria station and been met by Admiral Cumming's man, Clifford.

John had gone home and Richard had been put up in the same hotel as last time, both with instructions to report at nine sharp the next morning to Whitehall. Clifford had met them at the check point, escorted them to the fifth floor and shown them to the Admiral's office through an untitled door marked only with the number six.

He had greeted them warmly, offered them tea and invited them to sit down. The room itself was reminiscent of a captain's cabin with numerous seascapes on the wall, a brass telescope on the desk and an ancient log book sitting all by itself on a reader's podium.

The Admiral's desk was made of oak and pitted with scars and scrapes and looked a couple of hundred years old, which it probably was.

"Gentlemen, I was delighted to get your wire from Scapa and I look forward eagerly to your report. Please start at the beginning and go on until you come to the end, then stop."

Richard smiled at this quotation from Alice in Wonderland and began. He and John took it in turns for an hour and a half, interrupted only by the teapot being refilled. John finished and they both looked at the Admiral who had kept absolutely quiet throughout. Cumming got up from his chair to stretch his leg and stood gazing down at Whitehall for a moment. He sat down again and looked at each of them in turn.

"Gentlemen, I am deeply impressed. You have both done a magnificent job in an extremely difficult situation. Frankly, I didn't expect you to succeed, or even come close. I was obeying the king's wishes and making a gesture. That you failed in your task was caused only by the refusal of the Tsar to accompany you. I am sure that His Majesty will be deeply appreciative when I tell him."

"What do I do now, sir?" John asked. "Report back to the Met?"

"No." For the time being, Cumming was going to be evasive. "First, I want you both to write up a report on this. You can do it singly or jointly, whichever you prefer.

I spoke with His Majesty on the telephone this morning, telling him that you were back and he asked me for a report as soon as possible. I'd like it by tomorrow. Then both of you get lost until next Monday. A week's leave, do what you like, you've earned it. All expenses will be borne by this department, within reason.

Next Monday, I want you both back here for interrogation. I will have a number of people here who will be very interested in your impressions of Russia and the people you met. It will probably take about two days. Now, about this American Bulloch, where is he now?"

"At my hotel." Richard told him. "He's on his way back to Washington and I promised him some sightseeing before he leaves. I would like to emphasize his help in this affair. He saved my life once and helped us on the final stage in getting the cars to the pick up point."

"Yes, I understand. Do you think that he would appreciate a discreet note to President Wilson? A sort of thank you note for his co-operation."

"I'm sure he would, sir. It might do him a lot of good with the President."

"One other thing," Cumming said. "The Russian, Cherkassy. What became of him"

"He disappeared, sir." Richard told him. "We were all together on the train down from Scotland. We stopped at Crewe for about twenty minutes and got out to stretch our legs. When we returned to our compartment, he had gone.

He left a short note on my seat. It only said that he thought it would be better if he left now and hoping that perhaps we might meet in the future. I think that he's probably in Paris by now."

"Pity." The Admiral sighed. "Our boys would have dearly loved to talk to him about the Russian army, it's leaders and it's future plans."

"I think that may be why he left, sir." John told him. "Cherkassy foresaw that our Intelligence people would want to question him and decided that he would just as soon not answer any questions."

"Why not? He left Russia voluntarily. I would think that he would be happy to help us."

"Yuri's more complicated than that." Richard said. "He's out for himself, but at the same time, in his own way, he a loyal Russian. We talked a bit on the boat coming back. He thinks that the war will be over in a year, maybe less, and when it does, Russia will once again be the poor man of Europe. In his view, Russia has been dragged kicking and screaming into the twentieth century, and he thinks that the allies will be happy to see it go back to nineteenth again. He doesn't want that to happen. I think that you will probably hear from him again, if he lives long enough."

Mansfield Cumming rose and limped around his desk to shake both their hands again.

"Thank you both gentlemen. I assure you that the parts you played will not be forgotten. Now, go off and enjoy yourselves for a week. I'll see you both next Monday."

Kestrel and Cromwell left together leaving Cumming alone for a moment. Clifford entered and gathered up the tea things. He paused before leaving with the tray.

"Are you really going to send them back to their old jobs, sir?"

Cumming looked at him, surprised. His bushy white eyebrows lifted and he laughed shortly.

"Of course not! These were two amateurs, we threw them in at the deep end and they learned to swim. They have a natural talent and they work well together. I'm not about to throw them away. We have plenty of army captains and plenty of policemen, we don't have an unlimited supply of good intelligence officers. I'm going to give them this week to rest and then I'll hit them after the debriefing next week."

—

Clifford closed the door behind him and walked down the hall with the tea tray. He reflected that the Admiral in his way, was a ruthless man. He had a menu of different objectives and he would use anyone who he thought could achieve those objectives. Cumming always got his own way. He could be nasty or charming, whichever suited his book. He looked forward to welcoming two new colleagues into the secret world.

In the Rising Sun in Highgate, Kestrel and Cromwell toasted each other with a pint each of beer.

"What are you going to do now?" Richard asked.

"Right now I'm off to see my parents. They live not far from here, which is why I suggested this place. My father will be very interested in my travels."

"I don't think that's a very good idea." Richard told him. "Perhaps it was an oversight, but I expected the Admiral to warn us not to talk to anyone about it."

"You know, it's funny," John told him, "I remember thinking in Petrograd that London was some far off place that I knew vaguely and now that I'm here, I think of Petrograd in the same way."

Richard smiled, "I know what you mean. For six weeks we were caught up in the affairs of people far away from here. We were like a stone cast into the water. For a little while we made some ripples, but now the ripples have gone away and they can get back to making their own plans without our interference."

Richard sketched a large circle in the air. "Think of it. Here we are in this part of the planet sipping our beer in peace and quiet. Across the channel, only a few miles from here is a different world where it's kill or be killed." His finger moved on the imaginary globe. "And up here in Russia, It's plot and counter plot with a whole Country as the prize." His hand erased the world. "Will you join Lucius and myself for dinner tonight? Come over to the hotel about seven."

"I'll be there." John promised. "What about you? What will you do now?"

"After I see Lucius off on the boat on Wednesday, I'm going to stay with an aunt in Devon. I'm going to sit and do absolutely nothing for the rest of the time. Write a letter to my father in America, carefully not mentioning that I've been in Russia."

He took some of his beer and his eyes looked around the pub.

"God! It seems like a dream doesn't it? At the same time we've changed, you and I. We're not the same people anymore. I suppose that after we do this debriefing I'll be sent back to my regiment and you will be back to locking up villains. In a way, I'll miss it, won't you?"

Kestrel fleetingly thought of being arrested last month in Tsarskoe Selo and expecting to be shot.

He thought of driving the train in that last attempt and smiled briefly.

"Well, maybe a little." He conceded. "Are you writing to anyone else in America?"

Cromwell's face clouded. They had spoken of this before. There was a girl in Washington. They had met at a social affair. In a week he was in lust, in two he was in love and he thought she was as well. They had quarreled over his decision to join the colors then had tearfully made up.

"I was young and foolish. I thought I had to prove something to myself. Russia taught me a sharp lesson. I don't know, I told her not to wait."

"Don't be so stiff upper lip." John advised. "Write her, perhaps that's all she's waiting for."

"Damn the war." Richard said. "Who knows when I'll ever get back again?"

"When do you want to get to that report?"

"Right, I had forgotten. Why not come over to the hotel earlier and we'll start work on it."

Cromwell and Kestrel rose and went into the watery sunshine of a London afternoon. For a second, they stood at the entrance of the pub before going their separate ways. John turned to Richard.

"It was a hell of an adventure, wasn't it?"

Richard laughed and looked up at the sky before looking back at John.

"It sure as hell was."

POSTSCRIPT

IN OCTOBER OF 1917, Lenin finally achieved his life's aim. The second Russian Revolution put the Bolsheviks in power where they stayed for the next seventy years.

Alexander Kerensky fled Russia. First to Paris, then to America where he lived until his death.

The Tsar and his family were murdered on July 14, 1918. In Ekaterinburg, one year later.

Yuri Cherkassy was involved in the civil war that raged in Russia until 1921. He flirted briefly with The Trust, an anti-Bolshevik organization raising funds for the civil war until he realized that it had been set up by Feliks Derzhinsky as a front. He became quite wealthy, running his various shady operations from his villa in the south of France. He met Cromwell and Kestrel twice in the next twenty years.

Admiral Mansfield Cumming split Britain's Intelligence operations into two parts. Domestic and Foreign. Domestic was run out of room five next door to his office in room six. Later known as MI5 and MI6.

John Kestrel and Richard Cromwell resigned their positions in the police and the army. They worked in Six for twenty- five years, often together.

In Washington in 1919, in Amsterdam in 1922 and again in Leningrad in 1930. John was killed during the blitz on London in 1940. He received the George Medal for his heroic action on that occasion. Richard Cromwell retired from the Service in 1950. He and his wife spent their last years in the Bahamas.

Printed in the United States
31117LVS00001B/55-102